About Natalie Anderson

Natalie adores a happy ending, which is why she always reads the back of a book first. Just to be sure. So you can be sure you've got a happy ending in your hands right now—because she promises nothing less. Along with happy endings, she loves peppermint-filled dark chocolate, pineapple juice and extremely long showers. Not to mention spending hours teasing her imaginary friends with dating dilemmas. She tends to torment them before eventually relenting and offering—you guessed it—a happy ending. She lives in Christchurch, New Zealand, with her gorgeous husband and four fabulous children.

If, like her, you love a happy ending, be sure to come and say hi on facebook/authornataliea and on Twitter @authornataliea, or her website/blog: **www.natalie-anderson.com**

Waking Up
In The Wrong Bed

Natalie Anderson

MILLS
BOON

First published in Great Britain 2012
by Mills & Boon, an imprint of Harlequin (UK) Limited,
Eton House, 18-24 Paradise Road, Richmond, Surrey TW9 1SR

© Natalie Anderson 2012

ISBN: 978 0 263 22738 3

Harlequin (UK) policy is to use papers that are natural, renewable and recyclable products and made from wood grown in sustainable forests. The logging and manufacturing process conform to the legal environmental regulations of the country of origin.

Printed and bound in Great Britain
by CPI Antony Rowe, Chippenham, Wiltshire

Also by Natalie Anderson:

First Time Lucky?
Nice Girls Finish Last
Dating and Other Dangers
The End of Faking It
Walk on the Wild Side
Unbuttoned by Her Maverick Boss*
Caught on Camera with the CEO*
To Love, Honour and Disobey

*Part of the *Hot Under the Collar* duet

**Did you know these are also available as eBooks?
Visit www.millsandboon.co.uk**

MORAY COUNCIL LIBRARIES & INFO.SERVICES	
20 34 04 45	
Askews & Holts	
RF RF	

For June—
thank you for giving us such a great port
in our ground-shuddering storm.
We would have been lost if it weren't for you.

CHAPTER ONE

SOME wicked time beyond midnight, Ellie darted along the hallways of the luxury lodge in an almost sheer slip. The plush carpet absorbed the rapid beat of her bare feet. The puff of air-conditioning didn't cool the mad heat blushing her skin. She was on an indulgence mission and, imprisoned by hedonistic—champagne-riddled—impulse, sanity didn't stand a chance.

She danced down the stairs to the next level, to where she knew he was sleeping. She counted the doors—one, two, three—and opened the next.

But his bedroom was empty. The dim light of an almost moonless night invaded through open curtains, revealing no body-sized lump in the bed. In fact it was so smooth it looked like a perfectly iced cake.

Disappointment dashed her spirits—because she wasn't hungry for cake. She was starving for something way more meaty than that. She'd gone fun-free for too long. So, inspired by the fabulosity of the location, she'd decided to hell with it and to take what he'd been offering for weeks. Until now she'd parried his flirtatious invites, unsure of his integrity. But here, in this most seductive location, what did anything matter but the moment? And this moment she wanted to enjoy some male, *physical*, attention. In a place as beautiful as this, surely fantasy could come true?

Yes. Having finally got the courage, she wasn't going to let fate confound her. Reckless joie de vivre bubbled again and she slipped back out to the hall. Maybe she'd counted wrong, or had the wrong side of the corridor? She pivoted one eighty and counted again. One, two three. Carefully she turned the handle of the fourth door.

Occupied.

Her over-wired senses instantly assimilated the signs—warmth, gentle, regular breathing, a light spiced scent. She quietly closed the door behind her. A couple of steps in she nearly stumbled over the shoe. The size said it all—a man's boot. This was the one, then.

The ten-inch gap in the curtains let in what light that waning moon threw. A gap that wide had to be deliberate—he must like to see the sun, moon and stars too. Smiling, she blinked to adjust her vision. Then, yes, in the wonderfully huge bed, she could just make out his laid-back shape, right in the centre. His dark hair contrasted against the white pillow, his face turned away from her. Then cloud crossed the moon, dulling the room to nothing but shades of black.

But she crept forward, heated inside and out.

'Hey,' she whispered. 'Are you asleep?'

Dumb question when she could hear the regularity of that breathing for herself.

'Hey,' she murmured again as she stretched across the bed, her hand out to touch...*skin.*

Oh, he was hot.

She snatched her fingers back, suddenly shy. Her heart bashed her ribs as adrenalin flooded, forcing a too-fast beat. She took a second to breathe, because never before had she slipped into the driver's seat like this. Her throat blocked, she could think of nothing else to say. But sensation—temptation—drove her closer. Despite the goosebumps popping over every inch of her skin, she burned.

She knelt on the bed, boldness returning the closer she got to his heat. Slowly, she slid her hand towards the point where the bed was depressed by the weight of one big, warm male. Her seeking fingers hit the boundary from cool cotton to hot body, but she pushed through her last nervousness, sliding her fingers up and over his hair-roughened skin.

Every cell inside her squeezed. The hit of pure pleasure from that smallest of touches surprised her. She'd not expected such excitement from so little. But perhaps this was about risk as well and she, who'd always been risk averse, was beyond excited already.

In daylight she found him perfectly resistible— they'd never even kissed. It had mainly been talk and suggestion—a way to help pass the boring bits at work. And there'd been more dull moments than anything recently—all paperwork, no perks. She'd hoped for job satisfaction this weekend, knew this was part of why she'd been offered the trip. But this place had her thoughts turning to the personal. Yes, now, up this close to his heat and that scent she'd never before noticed, she couldn't wait to discover him in this dark night.

His skin was warm, the breadth and obvious strength of his muscles another surprise. Who knew that beneath his customary too-trendy suits was a body of awesome size? Clutching one hand to her chest, she gently swept the other over his stomach, sliding the sheet down as she searched him out. He was completely naked and as a result only one word remained in her brain—*amazing*.

She was lost in her unrestrained exploration, so it was a few seconds before she sensed the change in him. Then she felt the ripple as, beneath skin, his muscles responded to her touch.

Stimulated.

She was emboldened by those signs, her reach went further, firmer. And her own excitement built as she realised the extent of his. It wasn't just with her hand that she touched him now. Bending, she pressed her mouth to his thigh. His hands lifted, his fingers thrusting through her hair, gently massaging. So her instinct had been right.

He was awake.

She knelt, lifting a knee across so she straddled him.

'Oh, yeah.' Sleep-rusted, hoarse, hungry, his voice sounded strange.

'Yeah,' she agreed with a breathy laugh, heart racing at her daring and his rising to the occasion so magnificently. 'You're okay with this?'

'Oh, yeah,' he repeated with a groan.

She felt his big release of air. Felt his hands firmly curve around her thighs. His fingers stroked over her skin, but with enough strength to keep her there.

He wanted her there.

She closed her eyes, letting her fingers feel him—that hot, stretched skin. Her sensuality exploded, extremely intense. The delight in discovering her recklessness would have such reward made her all the more liberated. In the past she'd been shy sexually—cautious, self-conscious, half afraid of doing something wrong or not being good enough. She'd never have dared this. But none of those feelings came into play now. Under the influence of lush surroundings, rich food and drink, this inky midnight and his rapid response, she simply didn't care. She felt too heavenly. Scent filled the warm darkness—a mix of the citrus of her shampoo and the spice of his soap. Not his usual aftershave. She guessed it was the guest soap. She made a mental note to find out the brand because it tantalised—encouraging her to taste.

Bending forward again, she brushed her hair over his skin as she kissed across his chest, finding one of his nipples to lick. She ran her hand down his abs. His muscles were rock solid. Hell, *all* of him was rock solid.

He pushed her shoulders so she sat up. His hands slid over her slip, over her belly to shape her breasts. He suddenly moved, lifting to pull the fabric from her. She raised her arms so he could take it over her head and toss it, she didn't care where. His hands slipped back to her butt, clutching her close—his touch possessive. She liked it. She also liked the thick part of him that she had one hand around. He stayed strained upwards, so his mouth teased her breasts as his fingers had for those too few delicious seconds before. She trembled—amazed that she could be so close so quick.

'If I'd known it was going to be like this,' she muttered hotly, 'I wouldn't have held back so long.'

She could have been having sex this good for the last two months—how had she been so blind to this chemistry?

He buried his face harder into her curves. Clutching her closer, kissing down her neck all the more passionately.

All this time her other hand had been curled into a tight fist, and tucked in the middle of that was something she knew they needed—*now*. She reluctantly let go of him to take the packet in both hands, tearing it open. Then she tried to get the thing to work.

'You have to help me with this,' she panted. Her fingers not getting the slippery rubber to roll down right.

He lay back, his hands pushed hers out of the way, but she bent, following the downward stroke of his fingers with her mouth. He hissed a curse—a whisper so stretched with desire it broke.

She laughed, delighted, and lost her last fragment of inhibition. The breathlessness, the haste, the heat, all turned her on to an extreme degree. He seemed to have the same reaction. His erection strained flat against his stomach. She straddled, shifting closer to him, letting her core rest just on the base of him, his tight balls just beneath her butt. She teased them both with tiny squeezes of her muscles, like little kisses from her intimate lips. The hard ridge of him was delicious torment on her sweet spot and grinding against him set her on an even faster track to ecstasy. Oh, yeah, now it was carnal, now it was *insane*. Never so raw and passionate and quick. He growled and firmly slid his big hand up her thigh, then forced his fingers between their bodies. She moaned, abandoned, as he used his thumb to tease her. He sat up to kiss her breasts again as he toyed with her, circling her rhythmically, occasionally slipping deep. She was dripping with desire, unashamedly writhing as he flicked his fingers, as he licked and kissed up to her neck, then down to her breasts again. Almost at the point of climax she pushed him back, her strength catching him by surprise. A loud smacking sound clapped in the room as she broke the seal of his mouth on her skin. He fell back on the mattress and she held him there with a hard hand on his shoulder.

'I want to do it,' she growled, grabbing his rigid length in a wide fist, hovering above him for one moment of ecstatic anticipation.

She gasped as she slid, instinctively clamping tight and twisting down on him. He roared and she felt his muscles flex. She smiled, thrilled he was as turned on as she. He arched uncontrollably again; whatever words he muttered were unintelligible.

She pressed her palms to his big, taut biceps for leverage, for control. Her fingers curled into the solid muscle as she began to ride him. Filled with limitless energy and endurance, she took him deeper and deeper, over and over. He was big and powerful and she loved having him beneath her. Oh, yeah, he was the most incredible ride. Perfect—big enough to fill her ravenous appetite—too big really. But that was exactly what she'd wanted—an extreme experience of pleasure.

His hands cupped her breasts, teasing her nipples between finger and thumb, until—mere seconds later—she lifted and sank on him too fast for him to keep grip, so he swept his palms over her curves, slipping down to her waist, smoothing the sudden slick of sweat over her body. And then his hands spread wide on her thighs, his fingers firmed, holding her soft flesh as tightly as she was gripping his biceps. Suddenly he thrust hard, meeting her in a massive movement. She roared with pleasure then, as the duel for dominance began. Her fingers curled deep into his, pressing down as he pushed up, ratcheting the friction. They drove hard, slamming together faster and faster, each forcing the other to ecstatic abandonment.

'So good, oh, so good,' she panted, almost inaudible. 'Oh, it's never been so good.'

So good it was only seconds before she came with a harsh, high cry. Only one more before he came hard after.

* * *

Rapid, jerky breathing filled her head—her own and his. Sensual joy surged through her in a final squeeze. If she had the energy she'd laugh. But she was sweaty and breathless and so zapped she was fast sinking into a lax, sleepy mass.

She heard footsteps—the clipping sound of high heels on concrete. A cough, then laughter rising up from the courtyard below the window. She froze. People were still up, still awake. Could have heard... The realization brought reality back with a crash.

The morning after hadn't been a very much thought-upon part of her plan. Now all the decisions came to her split-second: this would change nothing between them. They'd be colleagues who'd had a carefree kick together *one* night. That was all. She knew he flirted with every woman he met and that this would mean nothing to him. So it had to mean nothing to her too. She liked to think he'd keep his mouth shut. While in their industry hook-ups were common, this was her first. But she knew it would hardly become notorious news—there were people far more important than her for others to talk about. And she was not going to let this get ugly. It was over already.

She peeled her chest from his, preparing to slide off his body and get back to her own room. But he pulled her back against him. He was stronger than she'd thought he'd be. He was more everything than she'd thought he'd be.

'Stay.' A low, sleepy word—but a command none the less. His embrace tightened. Inescapable but so irresistible.

She hadn't expected this caring comfort either. He rolled them both in a smooth movement, settling them into a sleep position—still devastatingly intimate.

The moment of clarity she'd had before now melted in lax drowsiness as she physically melted back into his warm strength. He lifted a heavy leg over hers, his arms curled tighter—cradling her ultra-close. Consciousness slipped. Her muscles were spent, that yearning in her depths sated. The last thing she heard was another burst of laughter coming through the open window. A man's laugh. With the last fragment of conscious energy she frowned—she recognised that laugh.

Hours later she slowly woke to a low moan echoing in her ears. Her *own* moan as she released a breath that seemed to have been held for ever. Her heart was pumping, her skin—and other bits—damp and *so* hot. She was having the most vivid, gorgeous dream. She resisted opening her eyes, wanting to stay in the sizzling fantasy. And in that fantasy she was imprisoned in the arms of one very hot, hard body—part of that body was very, *very* hard. His fingertips gently brushed down her lower belly. The urge to flex her hips—to invite—was irresistible. As she rocked back against him she felt the rebellious ache in her muscles, but she didn't care. Not as the memories cleared—the wildness of that ride coming into focus. Not when his hips teased right back and his fingers went…

'Good morning.' His voice was less sleep-rusted than it had been last night, but it was still strange.

Ellie froze. Her heart stopped, totalling her oxygen supply. Then she spun, inadvertently trapping his hand between her legs. The molten-brown eyes intently focused on her weren't the pale green ones she'd expected.

'Oh, my God!' She jerked to a sitting position, trapping his hand all the more. Clutching the sheet to her chest with hands curled into claws, she squawked, utterly breathless, 'Who the hell are you?'

CHAPTER TWO

RUBEN THEROUX had never had a bedmate regret frolicking with him and he had no intention of breaking that record now. He didn't care that he hadn't a clue who his sexy intruder was. No, the question he'd spent the last twenty minutes musing over was what colour her eyes were. Now he knew. Cornflower blue and crazy big. And though shock had whitened her face, she was still the prettiest thing he'd woken to find in his bed. Then again, he hadn't woken to anyone in his bed in a while. Relationships and Ruben were like oil and water, and he'd been too busy in recent times for even a five hour fling. So maybe it wasn't surprising he'd spent so long studying the soft woman soundly sleeping—until he'd succumbed to the temptation to tease. And, oh, my, she was hot to tease.

'You're not Nathan.' Strangled sound emerged as she stated the obvious.

'No,' he answered calmly, not moving a muscle so as not to freak her out more. But who the hell was Nathan and how could she have made such a mistake?

'How can you not be Nathan?' she gasped.

Yeah, his thoughts exactly. 'Well.' He stated it quietly. 'This isn't Nathan's room. This is my room.' Literally. Every room in the place was his.

Her mouth opened and closed a couple of times. He waited—motionless—to see how this was going to go. She didn't seem to realise her thighs were sandwiching his hand in a hot, smooth vice and he wasn't going to make any sudden kind of movement. But the memory of those limbs straddling his hips wasn't helping him recover his equilibrium. All he could feel were those lush, strong curves. He wanted the rest of him to be in the midst of them again.

She flicked a wild glance around the room and then arrowed all her attention right back at him. 'But this has to be his room—I counted the doors. The other one was empty.'

He pressed his lips together to stop the chuckle sliding out because he didn't want to make the situation worse for her.

'Are you sure you're in the right room?' she asked, her eyes still shocked wide.

'Positive. I got in late last night.' He'd been so tired it had been all he'd been able to do to stumble from the shower straight to what was definitely *his* bed. 'I came to bed and then the best dream ever turned out to be real.'

Only his dream-turned-real lover was now turning fifty shades of red—embarrassment staining her skin in a swift sweep. Her murmurs of pleasure came back to him—her rough claim that she hadn't known it would be so good. Yeah. The sweetheart *had* made a mistake. She'd meant that passion for some other guy. A sharp claw of envy swiped his ribs, puncturing his enjoyment of his best ever wake-up. But it hadn't been some other guy who'd pleased her so much. It had been *him*.

'You're a guest here?' she asked in a low choked voice.

'Actually I—'

She didn't give him the chance to introduce himself; instead she launched into a monologue of mortification and panic. 'Oh, I can't believe this. I can't believe it. I'm so sorry. I am so, so sorry.'

Partly because he wanted to see her reaction, but mainly because he couldn't resist, he let his fingers stroke—just the once, so very gently—in the hot, damp prison she gripped them in.

The incessant apologies ended instantly on a breathless gasp. Her mouth reddened, her muscles tightened and her temperature sizzled. His eyes locked on hers, watching the blue go brilliant, then her black pupils absorbed that colour as they swelled super fast. Her flush deepened. He felt the spasms before she twisted, releasing him as she scuttled to the far edge of the bed.

'You don't need to apologise,' he said, wondering if he should be the one saying sorry now. But he couldn't quite regret it. She'd been waking up so wonderfully willing in his arms when she'd thought he was this Nathan, but just then? That had been a raw response to *him*. She was hot and hungry for *him*. As she'd been last night when *he'd* been the one to meet her demands.

A swift glance told him what he needed to know—there were no rings between those white knuckles. No guy had staked a permanent claim and the Nathan guy was a fool for not taking her to bed sooner. The woman was passionate and hungry, literally a dream lover.

He coughed to ease the constriction in his chest. 'I'm sorry I'm not Nathan.'

Only because he wanted what she'd meant for the other guy—that invitation and pleasure. Hell, he wanted it now. He was stiffer than a steel pipe and feeling her sensual response spike like that had worsened it. But he fought the impulse to drag her close again, wincing at his new-found Neanderthal leanings.

The poor woman was completely mortified and he was all rampaging lust, desperate to sleep with her again. What kind of human was he?

Definitely one who'd been without too long. Because try as hard as he could he couldn't seem to 'relax'.

'Don't be sorry.' She emphatically shook her head.

Her deepening discomfort bothered him more than his uncontrollable body. Somehow he had to limit the damage here and help her find a funny side. And nothing smoothed a situation more than some humour.

Ellie struggled to hide her breathlessness. Shock still had her lungs in a tight grip, but so did desire—she was seconds from orgasm and, frankly, that doubled her shock.

She stared at the complete stranger only a couple of feet from her. The stranger that she now knew so *intimately*. And just looking at him sent her heart rate through the ceiling.

'You're okay?' The soft query delivered between dangerously curved lips. That gorgeous smile was as natural to him as the stripes were to the tiger. Oh, yeah, he'd been blessed with beautiful lips, upturned at the ends so he looked as if he was always in good humour. Which, given all his other assets, he probably was.

She clutched the sheet closer. Only her action dragged the sheet completely off him and, yeah, this was definitely *not* Nathan. And his natural assets were…sizable.

'I'm so sorry this happened,' she said again, determined to ignore the savage desire rippling through her like some internal beast that refused to be tamed. What kind of depraved animal had she turned into?

'I'm not.'

She hardly heard him as she apologised another ten times, interspersing the phrase with a few more choice words beneath her breath. Clutching the sheet to her with one hand, she put her now freezing hand to her face.

He sat up, resting his weight on one hand behind him, and spoke more forcefully. 'You didn't do anything I didn't want you to.'

That silenced her for all of a second. 'You didn't have much choice.' She looked across the bed at him. 'I *seduced* you.' The guy had been sound asleep and she'd been stroking him all over. Like everywhere.

His smile burst forth again. 'Yeah, well, it wasn't like I said no.' He chuckled. 'And it wasn't like I was a virgin.'

Well, no, he hadn't been that. Ellie bit her lips to stop from smiling. He'd had all the moves. And he executed another now—a languorous stretch that drew her attention once more to his completely fit length.

Hell, she had to move away before she did something stupid again. So she stood, taking the sheet with her. She didn't care about leaving him exposed, he didn't seem to be bothered by it. Whereas all she wanted to do was *hide*. She tried to wind the sheet around herself, glanced up to see him watching close—with undisguised amusement—and arousal. Man, was he aroused.

'You're free to take advantage of me any time you like,' he said softly, lying back down again. 'Or, you can come back to bed and let me take advantage of you this time.'

Oh, she so nearly had already and they both knew it. She felt her blush deepen. 'I really am sorry.'

'Sweetheart,' he drawled, but with an underlying

hint of seriousness. 'I could have stopped you if I'd wanted to.'

And there was the question. She looked up from her twisted toga attempt—facing his gaze direct. 'Why didn't you want to?'

He roared with laughter, his whole body clenched into an expression of enjoyment. Her gaze skittered south all of its own accord. *Built* for enjoyment—his clearly defined muscles spelled strength and stamina and gloriously good reproductive genes. And his reaction proved he was *such* a man. An all-about-fun man. She'd been a sexual toy for the night—as of course he had been for her. A really *good* toy.

Ellie tried to get her thoughts back on track—berating herself with worst-case scenarios. Imagine if he'd been married. What if he hadn't been alone in the room? She didn't know which would be worse. All she knew was that his utterly relaxed acceptance of her mistake was astounding.

'What were you thinking going along with it? Do women leap on you all the time?' Actually, looking at him? They probably did.

'I was asleep. At first I thought it was just an amazing dream.'

'A 4D dream,' she said sceptically.

'Yeah, hot and wet,' he half groaned, movement rippling down his muscles. 'You're sure you don't want to come back to bed?'

'Quite sure.' She clipped out the lie, all of a sudden desperate to get out of there before she threw caution to the wind and went for a repeat of last night's decadence.

'Honey, relax. I'm single, you're...' He paused, his voice lifting in question, his eyes unwaveringly focused on hers.

'Single,' she confirmed.

He paused as his expression seemed to sharpen. 'So tell me about Nathan.'

'He's no one.' She so didn't want to go there.

'He's not your boyfriend or your benefits guy or whatever?'

'No.' She squeaked out an answer from her strangled-feeling throat. She supposed she did owe the guy some kind of explanation but it was just so mortifying. 'We're colleagues. He'd been flirting and I... For once I just felt like...' She trailed off, her toes curling into the plush carpet. Now she wanted to disappear into the sheet completely.

'Nothing wrong with feeling like it.' Her naked lover shrugged his shoulders. 'So it wasn't because you're secretly in love with the guy and want to have his babies?'

'No babies,' she answered faintly. 'Don't worry.' She inhaled a hit of oxygen for courage. 'What we did was... It was safe.'

He sat up slowly. 'I remember.' His gaze lingered on her mouth. 'So no babies but you're not in love with him either?'

She shook her head. 'I just thought I'd say yes for once. Take the bull by the horns, so to speak.'

'You like rodeo?' His irrepressible smile quirked.

'Actually I don't think it's really for me,' she muttered, all but dying.

'But you ride so beautifully. Great seat, great rhythm. You're a natural,' he teased, chuckling at her baleful look. 'So you don't often do random seductions?'

The idea of her being some vixen seductress was so far off the mark it was hysterical. But she wasn't going to get hysterical herself. No, she took a calming breath and reckoned she could manage to get into the tease zone too. That was the way to handle this. 'Only on full moons.'

'Oh, you're a were-woman?'

She flicked her brows and then dropped the pretence. 'Honestly, the location helped.' She fiddled with the sheet and couldn't look at him. She knew this guy of all guys wasn't going to get hung up on double standards, but she was still embarrassed.

'The *chateau*?'

'It's so luxurious.' She nodded, truly meaning it. 'All the fabric, the furnishings. It's beautiful.'

'Yeah,' he said slowly. 'But I've never thought of it as an *erotic* destination. It's not like there are mirrors on the ceiling, tie-me-down bed ends, or twenty types of massage oil in the bathroom cabinet.' He glanced around the utterly tasteful room with a perplexed look.

Ellie was smoking-hot over his list of essentials for an erotic destination. She'd never thought she'd be into anything more than vanilla but the man had said 'tie-me-down' and she was ready to hunt out the ropes. She banished the image but couldn't help smiling as she tried to explain it more. 'It has this kind of discreet decadence. And it was a warm night. I'd had the most amazing shower.' She put her hand to her head because this so wasn't enough. 'And they serve French champagne.'

'Ah-h-h.' He nodded as if that explained it all. 'French champagne.'

She shrugged and gave up at that. She truly hadn't been tipsy. She'd just been bewitched and decided to please herself.

'This place was once dubbed Frenchman's Folly, did you know that?' he asked softly.

'No.' She frowned. 'No one could call this place a folly. It's more a fantasy.'

And you had to have a fantastical bank balance to be able to stay here. A guy this fit was probably some elite athlete or something. She wondered if she ought to recognise him.

'Perhaps people thought his folly was his marriage.'

'Oh.' Ellie paused. 'Shame if he was heartbroken. This isn't a place for heartbreak.'

Her naked lover chuckled. 'Only for pleasure, huh? But you and your colleague were here for business?'

'I wasn't supposed to come here at all.' She flushed deeper at the unintended entendre. 'It's not one of my files but last minute our boss wanted me to be here for backup.'

'So what's the business?'

'I work as a location scout. You know—finding places to film movies and stuff.'

His brows lifted as he picked up her lack of enthusiasm. 'You don't think this would be a good location?'

'It would be an amazing location,' Ellie said fervently. 'And I know it sounds like an amazing job and all—it's actually really not that much fun.'

'How can having to spend time in places like this not be fun?' he challenged her.

'I don't get to come on the trips much.' She coloured again as she saw him smile. 'I'm usually stuck in the office working on the paperwork. I've not been there that long.' She shrugged. Trouble was she excelled at paperwork—every job she had she'd done too well in the admin department to be let out of it. Frustrating wasn't the word.

'And so to make sure you got the most out of this

trip, you went hunting for some pleasure as well?' He was laughing as he said it.

And what could she do? There was no hope in denying it or in explaining the mad moment of need for contact that she'd experienced. So she nodded. 'Massive mistake.'

'Yeah, but not a disaster.'

Not a disaster, no—she'd had the best sex of her life. But it had been with a total stranger. They hadn't even kissed. There was absolutely no emotional connection between them. It just wasn't supposed to work that way. And she couldn't want more—could she? She tried to claw back her common sense—because what kind of a guy happily screwed complete strangers? A playboy. With a smile that cheeky and attitude that cocky? Yeah, as he'd admitted, he was no innocent.

She closed her eyes and groaned. 'Why didn't I turn on the light?'

'Given the way you're clutching that sheet around you, I'm guessing you like it best in the dark.' He laughed. 'Typical.'

'Excuse me?' Indignance rose, she couldn't restrain her reaction to his tease.

'Hiding your body.' He shook his head. 'What a waste.'

There was some truth to his accusation. Lights on for sex wasn't something that did it for her—fast-train to self-conscious. And it was then that she became aware of what she must look like—no doubt her hair would be bigger and more bouffant than some eighties rockstar's. Oh, fabulous. At least she wouldn't have panda eyes from smudged mascara. But still, this didn't really make up for the fact that she'd slept with the wrong guy. The guy she couldn't tear her eyes from.

He was smiling as dangerously as ever. 'But then you clearly have a latent wild streak.'

It seemed so. But next time she felt in need of satisfaction she'd mail order a vibrator. She clamped her elbows to her ribs, holding the sheet in place while she tried to cool her cheeks with her hands. She was getting turned on all over again just by looking at the guy. 'Look, I really should go. Let's just forget this ever happened.'

She attempted a march to the door. Only her sheet was a liability and his nudity gave him a speed advantage.

'You don't get away just yet.' He leaned against the door blocking her exit, all six feet four inches of bared magnificence. 'We have some more to talk about.'

Now he was standing up and towering over her, she had the melting sensation so deep it was unbearable. Her fingers itched; she could hardly stand still against the hot pull inside. Secret muscles flexed in excitement. Her heart thundered.

'Will you put some clothes on?' she asked desperately. He was too damn *hot* and she couldn't think with him like that.

His amusement flared again. 'Why? I'm not going to hide how attracted I am to you.'

It wasn't *her* he was attracted to, it was sex. And his nudity was messing with her hormones too. She'd gone completely animal. She half laughed on a gasp. 'Just please put some clothes on. Please.'

He shrugged his refusal, his expression one of total tease. 'I'm comfortable. You're really not comfortable with baring all, are you?'

What she wasn't comfortable with was her body's insane reaction to the sight of his—tall, toned and so sex-ready her insides were curling in on themselves. Her nerves clamoured for the sensation of him sliding in and out of her. This complete stranger had her more insanely excited than she'd ever been in her life. 'Well, can you please turn around while I get decent?'

'Really?' His full lips pouted. 'I don't get the peep show?'

'You've had more than enough, okay?' she choked. 'Please be the gentleman I know you are and turn around.'

'What makes you so certain I'm a gentleman?'

She fearlessly held eye contact. 'You let the lady go first.'

'Oh, that wasn't gentlemanly. That was for my own pleasure.' His lips curved more deeply into that delicious smile and he answered mock primly, 'But, okay, if you insist, I shall avert my eyes.'

He presented her with his rear view. She just gawped for a second, before remembering her intention and dropping the sheet to hurriedly dash back across the room, around the bed to find her slip. Glancing down, she saw a couple of light bruises colouring her thigh. The faintest of finger marks. She remembered his firm clutch with vivid clarity. The squeezes as she'd slid down to take him to the hilt over and over. She turned her head away and screwed her eyes shut tight, as if she could block the blush as the involuntary excitement skittered through her.

'Okay, I'm decent.' Breathing in, she watched him turn back to face her. He was no more physically 're-laxed'.

'You were wearing *that*?' He half gasped, theatrically pressing his hand against his ribs. 'Damn, I wish you *had* turned on the lights.'

'Stop it.' She laughed. 'You don't need to try and flatter me.'

'Yeah, I do.' He walked towards her, totally serious now. 'How can I not?'

She could see the muscles twitching under his skin. She'd never considered herself any kind of seductress before and she knew she wasn't really now—it was that sexual toy thing. They shared an illicit fantasy for real. The guy was no doubt sex-mad. Insatiable. One track. Only problem with that was his condition had rubbed off on her. Hell, the thought of him finding her so attractive put a zing in her step. But to do this again— stone-cold sober and in the cold light of day? She wasn't that *crazy*. She backed up, snatched up the towel from the low table next to her and threw it at him in defence.

He caught it and held it so it unfolded like a flag. 'What am I supposed to do with this?'

Oh, hell, she'd not got the towel—only the facecloth that had sat on top of it. Pocket-hanky-sized—ridiculously small hanging from his hand.

'I'm insulted,' he teased. 'I think you need a refresher in what I have to offer.'

'Oh, don't.' She giggled, unable to hide her all-over-body blush in just the slip—she needed the sheet back. 'Just…don't.'

He chuckled. 'I'm glad you can see the funny side.'

Biting her lip, she shook her head. 'Oh, this is such a nightmare.'

'Crazy, yes, nightmare, no. Don't regret it.'

She steadfastly met the sincerity in his eyes. And the smile on his mouth. Yeah, she bet he'd experienced many a morning after. 'You know how to give a girl a good time.'

'I like to think it's one of my strengths.'

Oh, it was.

He turned, his attention grabbed by something out of the window. 'This Nathan guy,' he muttered. 'Wouldn't have dark hair and laugh like a hyena?'

She reluctantly moved to stand next to him. Not a hyena, but a distinctive laugh. She remembered hearing it late last night, right when she shouldn't have. Right when she'd breathlessly been falling towards sleep, when her lover had still been inside her and caressing the base of her spine with gentle fingers.

'Oh.' She swallowed the swearword when she saw Nathan kiss the pretty young woman they'd met at the bar in the late afternoon yesterday.

Naked Guy's eyebrows had shot upwards. 'It looks like he might have been sharing his flirt around.'

Just a little.

'It's like a French farce,' Ellie muttered. But it was real. 'In a chateau and everything.' She felt her mystery lover turn his gaze on her and refused to show any kind of disappointment.

'I can't believe you mistook me for him,' Naked Guy accused in a tone of utter outrage. 'He's at least five inches shorter than I am. And not as fit.' He flexed his muscles in a preening display.

Yeah, they were poles apart. This guy was way more outrageous than Nathan. Bold in flirtation. In his demands. Desire. He tempted with humour and cheerful abandon.

'You were lying down,' she said through gritted teeth.

'And you hadn't slept with him.' He sounded pleased about that.

She didn't reply. She knew she'd admitted that last

night in her amazed gasps of pleasure. They both watched the couple in the courtyard for another moment.

Her tall lover was the one to break the silence, turning to face her directly. 'Well, I'll be frank, I think you got the better deal.'

She gaped at him. Then giggled. 'Arrogant much?' She laughed again only for the sound to die quickly as she shook her head and gave it to him. 'But I'll admit in this case, I think you might be right.'

'You *think*?' he asked, mock-outraged. 'Come on, you know that was spectacular.'

She felt her blush rising again as memories twisted between them, trying to draw them together.

'Well.' She breathed out, brazening her way through the most mortifying experience of her life. 'Okay. Yes. Thanks so much, it was…' She couldn't think of an appropriate adjective.

'Fantastic and you can't wait to see me again,' he inserted for her.

She shook her head. 'No.' She tempered the bad news with a smile. 'This was what it was.' One almighty screw-up. 'But we're not going there again.'

'Oh, come on.' He walked forward. 'That hot, that quick?' He shook his head. 'We'd be crazy not to enjoy that again. You want to as much as I do.' His gaze flickered to her chest. She didn't need to look down to know her nipples were turned on like bright beacons, begging for his touch again.

Oh, yeah, she was tempted.

'It had been a while for you, hadn't it?'

'Last full moon,' she said breathlessly.

'Liar.' He called her on it. 'You're blushing more than a gaggle of schoolgirls. You can hardly look at me. You're no vixen. Although it has to be said you have potential.'

She rolled her eyes. 'And you're offering to give me a bit more practice?'

'Of course I am,' he said simply. 'It had been a while for me too.'

She snorted. That she simply didn't believe.

His grin flashed. 'Truth. I've been busy at work and I haven't had any midnight callers. But you've really whet my appetite.'

Had she? It wasn't only his appetite piqued.

'I know it was an unconventional way of meeting, but we're good together.'

For a moment Ellie let fantasy rule—imagined being with him again for another round or thirty of spectacular sex. Fantasy morphed—from this they'd develop some wonderful relationship that would rival the highest-grossing Hollywood chick flick's happiest of endings… And, yeah, there was the problem. In the past she'd given too much where it wasn't wanted. She'd been crushed before; she wouldn't be daft enough to set herself up for a similar sort of heartache. She knew herself, before long she'd want the full fantasy. But a guy like this wasn't the sort to do happy ever after. She'd seen his unveiled edge—unashamed, reckless—a complete playboy. Someone who could go along with an anonymous one-night stand with such relaxed, outrageous humour? Too, *too* casual. And while she could live with a casual—frankly marvellous—mistake in her life, it had to be one-off. Her non-plan with Nathan had been for just the once. This *definitely* had to be just the once. Naked Guy here was just too fit for her to keep up with.

'It can't happen.' Her final decision.

'Not because of Nathan.' Statement not question.

'No. Because of me.' She'd get burned by Mr Naked & Too Hot to Handle. He was too much more everything than any other man she'd met—more gorgeous, more good-humoured, not only blessed by nature but more talented in bed than any guy had the right to be. She'd fall so hard, in a heartbeat.

He hadn't taken his eyes from hers, as if trying to read her thoughts. Looking right back at him, into those molten-chocolate eyes, Ellie felt her thoughts begin to splinter dangerously. One thought became dominant. Not a thought—an *urge*. Steam rose, blinkering her vision—all she wanted was to plant a kiss on those perfectly curved lips.

She breathed, blinked, stepped back. Not going to happen. She moved quickly, opening the door and stepping out of the insanity.

'Wait.' He stepped after her, apparently not caring that she was in the middle of the hall in a sheer slip and he had only a facecloth failing to protect his modesty. 'I don't know your name. Mine's—'

'Don't.' She held up her hand. 'Let's just pretend the whole thing was a dream.'

'But—'

'Bye!' She clutched her breasts so she could sprint down the hallway to the stairs.

'You're going to leave me like this?'

She turned at his holler, saw him standing outrageously proud, bolder than anyone she'd met in her life. He had a fascinating lack of care, and an ability to find amusement in anything—that made him all the more

intriguing. But she forced another step back from temptation. 'I'm sure you'll figure something out.'

Yeah, it'd be no time 'til he tempted another woman
into his bed. And Ellie would be all envy.

CHAPTER THREE

'ELLIE, where have you been?' Nathan pointedly looked at his watch when Ellie finally made it down to the breakfast table an hour and a shower later. There was no sign of his girl guest—or any other guests either.

She squared her shoulders, refusing to feel even a hint of regret about last night. Maybe she should feel worse, but the gorgeous Naked Guy had completely diffused any threat of angst with his humour and relaxed attitude. And Nathan here had been scoring someone else. At least *he* never had to know about her crazy intention last night. She really had got the better end of the deal.

'I've been waiting ages for you.' Nathan's tone turned more to the 'smooth' one he used so often.

And she really didn't think so. 'I didn't know we were in such a rush to get going,' she answered ultra matter-of-factly.

'We're not leaving.' Nathan surprised her. 'He's here.'

'Who?'

'The owner. He's turned up unexpectedly.'

'The French guy?' Son of the folly man? Given the old dude hadn't lived to see the chateau finished, she guessed the son to be in his late forties or fifties.

Nathan nodded vehemently. 'We have to do whatever it takes to convince him this is the place.'

Ellie didn't want to stay here a moment longer than necessary, not when she had that other guest to avoid. Besides, securing permission to film onsite wasn't usually a problem. Business owners were thrilled to get the exposure. Plus they were well compensated. Although this place was in a class of its own. The elite of the elite retreated here where every luxury was on tap—and the key was its privacy. 'What's your plan?'

Nathan was frowning at her outfit. 'I thought you might toy with the man or something?'

'Pardon?' Ellie asked, certain she'd heard wrong.

'You know, charm him.' He was still frowning at her outfit. 'Flirt him round your finger.'

Ellie blinked as the real Nathan was revealed. Yeah, now the smooth had been removed—she realised that was what *he* did. Oozed charm to get what he wanted. All those compliments and the coy flirting he'd done with her? What had he really been after? Clearly not sex. She'd known the industry she worked in was all about the illusion—but this was killing the dream too much for her. 'We might work for film-makers, but the casting couch doesn't happen when it comes to *locations.*'

Lying back in bed—still recovering from his interrupted sleep—Ruben was glad for the open window and the way words spoken in the courtyard were carried up to his ears. The conversation going on down there was supremely interesting.

'He's French, isn't he? Frenchmen love an elegant woman. Not sure they like jeans.'

'Actually denim was originally created in France,'

Ellie—Ruben liked her name—snapped back at the Nathan prat.

'Well, don't you have anything sexier? What about a skirt or something?'

'I don't think skin is going to get us far. He's probably married.'

Ruben bit back a chuckle at that suggestion.

'Can't you make the effort? This is a major deal—you know that, don't you?'

'I'm not going to prostitute myself just to land a contract, Nathan. That's not the way I operate.'

'You know this industry is *all* about image,' Nathan lectured her. 'I wanted you here because you're so boringly together with paperwork, but you have to step up to the plate when the heat is on.' Nathan began with the clichéd metaphors. 'You need the killer instinct. You do whatever it takes to impress him.'

Ruben couldn't believe she'd wanted to get it on with this idiot. What had she been thinking?

'You might flirt your way into getting what you want, but that's not what I'm about,' Ellie answered back.

Go, the spitfire.

'Don't you want to win?' the doofus asked.

'Not at that price,' she answered smartly.

No, he'd known she wasn't ruthless or cynical. Ruben frowned at the hint of real hurt in her tone. Had she really had feelings for the jerk?

'Fingers crossed the guy is gay, Nathan, so you can be the one to flash the skin.'

Ruben got out of bed and walked into his bathroom. He couldn't wait to get down there. But by the time he did, she was alone, the only sign of any lingering an-

noyance the light flush on her cheeks. A flush that deepened when she saw him.

'Good morning,' he said to her for the second time
that day.

'Oh.' She looked startled he'd spoken, as if she'd
thought he was a mirage or something. 'Hello.'

Ms Cautious herself.

'You never mentioned your plans this morning.' He
walked to the table that was laden with breakfast op-
tions. 'It's a beautiful place—are you going to explore
it some more?'

She shook her head and looked everywhere but at
him. 'I'm here to work.'

'But you don't much like your work. You're supposed
to come here to relax and escape. Have you hunted out
the spa facilities yet?'

Her flush deepened again. 'I don't have time for the
spa. I really have to work and I really do need to get
on with it so…'

'Maybe you ought to have some breakfast first. You
must be hungry after last night.'

He sat down at the table, aware of the frustrated look
she directed at him. No, he wasn't going to leave her
alone. He bit into a croissant to hide his smile.

'I think I'll just have a coffee.'

He reached for the pot before she did, pouring a cup
and handing it to her with deliberate care.

'Thanks,' she mumbled.

Ruben sent her a hot look. He didn't like her reserve;
he preferred the tease he'd seen up in his room. And
he knew there was a bomb going off behind that frozen exterior.

'Ruben Theroux!' a guy called loudly, striding out

from inside, a huge smile on his face. 'Wonderful to see you.'

Ruben knew the difference between sycophantic and genuine warmth. This was a no-brainer. He glanced at Ellie—a total 'what were you thinking?' look. Then he turned back to Nathan.

'I'm sorry, I'm not sure who you are,' Ruben answered coolly, not bothering to stand, just looking up from the table.

But clearly Nathan had done his homework—unlike his sidekick.

'I'm Nathan, I'm here with CineSpace. You know we're interested in your fabulous property. It would be just perfect for—'

'I'd like to finish my breakfast first,' Ruben interrupted, blatantly dismissive. 'Perhaps we can talk later?'

'Oh.' Nathan rallied in less than a second, his reply too collegial. 'Of course.'

'Why don't you go down to the stables? I'll be sure to find you there.'

Having sent the pain in the neck away, Ruben looked at the stop-sign-red face of his curvy midnight caller and felt that foreign tug in his chest again. To cover the awkward moment he went for the usual—tease. 'So, what are you going to do next to impress me?'

Ellie forced back the faint feeling. The guy she'd slept with was the owner Nathan reckoned she had to 'do anything to impress'—and he'd *listened in* to that conversation?

'How else?' Her temper flared. Did he think last night had been her attempt at the casting couch? 'Look, I didn't know who you were. It was a genuine—'

His laughter cut her off. 'I know that, sweetheart. I got in really late, no one knew until this morning that

I was here. I know you weren't trying to convince me to say yes in time-honoured fashion.'

She still didn't believe he was the owner. 'You're supposed to be French.'

'I'm half French but I've lived in New Zealand since I was six.'

'You're not old enough to own this place.' He looked late twenties. Dressed in jeans and a tee he looked more like the gardener than the owner. But that fitting-too-good tee shirt had 'Lucky' emblazoned across his chest and Ellie already knew the guy got lucky—every, single, time.

'My father was an old man when I was born.'

And he'd had a folly of a marriage? To a much younger woman? Ellie decided to skip that can of worms—she had a huge enough one open already. 'You told me you were a guest.'

'You assumed that. I did try to explain who I was but you were too busy apologising to listen.'

'I'm not going to apologise any more,' she said defiantly. 'You should have told me. You should have stopped me making a fool of myself twice over.'

He stood and walked around to her side of the table. 'You never made a fool of yourself with me.'

She stood, speaking through a clamped jaw. 'Mr Theroux.'

He stepped closer. 'You can't be serious.' His voice dropped to an intimate whisper.

'Actually I am,' she declared firmly, shoring up her quivering response. 'You know it's inappropriate for us to talk further. You need to talk to—'

'Nathan.'

'That's right.' She inhaled—bad idea because she caught that deliciously spicy soapy scent.

'I don't want to deal with Nathan. I want to deal with you.'

Now she knew what menopause was going to feel like: the hot flash stunned her. 'You can't.' She snuck a breath. 'It would be unprofessional. Nathan will work on it alone.'

'There's nothing to work on.' He shrugged.

'Are you saying that because I'm leaving, you're not interested in negotiating?' she asked even more breathlessly. 'Are you trying to blackmail me?'

He hesitated. 'I'm open to negotiations. But I would prefer to talk with you.'

'But if I'm not available will you still be open?'

He grinned. 'I'm a businessman, not an idiot. I know there are benefits to be had from this place being used as a location. Not for just any movie, of course.'

She gazed at him through narrowed eyes. Not sure she could believe him.

'I enjoyed every second with you in my bed, but I'm not slimeball enough to use our fling in my business decisions,' he said quietly but firmly. 'Just as you're not slutty enough to think sleeping with me could make me change my mind, right?'

'Right,' she said. 'But the fact is we don't know each other very well.'

'And as far as you're concerned we're not going to get to know each other any better.'

'I think that's best, don't you?'

'Not at all,' he answered bluntly. 'But unlike your colleague I'm gentleman enough to respect your wishes. I'm not into harassing people.'

Just how much of that conversation with Nathan had he overheard?

'I'm capable of keeping my business and my personal life separate,' he continued easily. 'It won't make any difference.'

Well, he was more capable of that than she was—she couldn't think straight with the guy around.

'Truth is I'm in the midst of a new deal to take on two new boutique hotels so a cash injection plus publicity could be useful. That's why I'm more open to film negotiations now than I was a couple of months ago.'

'Well, you'll need to talk to Nathan. I no longer work for the location company.'

Utterly silent, he stared—his brown eyes shifting to black and hard in a whisker of a second. 'You got the *sack*?'

Ellie shivered in the face of iced fury. The ultimate in easy-going humour had a frozen fiery depth she hadn't anticipated. Ruben Theroux wasn't someone to make angry. And now she knew he hadn't listened in to the whole conversation she'd had with Nathan.

'Nathan didn't have the authority to sack me. I resigned,' she said, lifting her chin. 'With immediate effect.'

His jaw dropped. 'Why?' Now he looked even more angry. 'You're just going to quit and run from some silly little mess?'

It wasn't a silly little mess. It wasn't anything to do with Ruben. She'd seen the light. She'd been taken on by that company to keep the paperwork tidy and to flooze where necessary. She might be a complete pleaser but that was taking it too far.

He glanced down at her clothes—and, no, her jeans weren't designer like his. Hers had frayed at the edges from use, not been bought that way.

'What are you going to do?'

Pride surged. 'I'm not so stupid to throw in a job

without having something else lined up. It's all sorted already. I start next week.'

'Doing what?'

She didn't want to tell him the finer details—not that she was embarrassed, more that she sensed it would be safer to keep him distanced. He was in her 'past' already. 'Same industry, different job.'

'You've got a part in a film, then?' He suddenly grinned. 'Lead role?'

'No.' She bit back an answering smile. 'I'm not a wannabe actress.'

'But you have leading-lady looks.'

She vehemently shook her head. 'Please not the flirting again.'

'It's impossible not to,' he murmured. 'Come on, tell me.'

She shook her head. 'Not acting.'

'That's really not a fantasy?' he scoffed. 'Any woman who works in the industry has that fantasy.'

'Well, I don't. I can't think of anything worse than being judged harshly on a giant screen.'

He gave her a sideways look. 'Well, you got your new job organised pretty quick.'

'She's been after me for some time.' It was true. She'd only had to send a text asking Bridie if she was still keen and the emphatic 'yes, start Monday' had been received less than a minute later. 'I've been mulling it a while.'

Fact was she was tired of trying to please everyone— and of not progressing.

Ruben Theroux still looked troubled. Ellie's pride bit deeper. 'Don't think that my decision has anything to do with what happened with you.'

'It doesn't?'

'I've been thinking of a change for months.'

'You're not letting that Nathan drive you out, are you?' he asked carefully. 'Because he's not worth it. Trust me, no relationship is worth killing your career for.'

'You know this from personal experience?' she asked, happy to get the focus on him for a change.

'Possibly.' He shrugged. 'Just don't let anyone get in the way of what you want to achieve.'

'Okay.' She laughed, not needing the 'best friend' advice from her random-stranger lover. 'Actually I feel liberated.'

She wanted the fun back—to be involved in the industry where she was among her own kind: the fans. And that was what Bridie was offering her. They'd met one day at a location—Bridie took fans on set tours, and she knew just how much of a movie buff Ellie was.

'How liberated are you feeling?' Ruben Theroux's expression had sharpened.

Already she knew what that gleam meant. 'Not that liberated.'

'There's absolutely no conflict of interest now.'

'That's definitely not why I resigned.'

'But you know that, despite everything, we never did kiss.'

'We did a whole lot more than kiss.'

He shook his head. 'But we never kissed mouth to mouth. I remember that clearly. I've spent the last hour remembering every second we had, very clearly.'

She mirrored his head-shake. 'We're not going to kiss now.'

'You can't tell me you're afraid.'

His whisper stirred right where she refused to be stirred. 'You can't try to tease me into it.'

It wasn't right that she have the best sexual experience of her life with a complete stranger. One who'd no doubt share himself with the rest of the female population given half the chance. She convinced herself it had been so amazing because she'd been without so long. She'd been celibate for so many months, it had been like a cork releasing from an all-shook-up bottle of champagne. But these things didn't last. Another sip and she'd discover how flat it had gone. It had to be that one-off pop of pleasure.

'I think we should try just the once, just to see.' A winning, teasing, tempting smile.

She laughed. It was very apparent that Ruben Theroux wasn't used to having his plans thwarted. He got what he wanted. And while part of her wanted what he was offering, she knew she'd want more than what he was prepared—or even able—to give in the long run.

'No.' She could say that to him and mean it. Sure she could.

'There's nothing so simple as a kiss.'

'And nothing so complicated.' And unfortunately, nothing else she could think about. His lips caused the problem. That natural curve upwards made them so inviting. Then there was that screamingly masculine line to his jaw. And those wretchedly captivating, laughing eyes.

'Well, if you're sure...' He extended the invitation another few seconds.

'Thanks anyway.' She stepped back from it, turned and fled.

Up in her room it took all of thirty seconds to fling her things into her overnight bag. She giggled at the thought of his temptation. Terribly gorgeous guy, bound to be terribly unreliable.

He was waiting round the front of the chateau. Her car had been brought up by one of those invisible service people who were brilliant.

'I'll make sure Nathan gets home somehow,' Ruben said with a faint grimace.

'Shouldn't you be off talking with him already?' She stowed her bag in the backseat.

'He's not my number one priority at the moment.'

'Oh, you're so good at the flattery, aren't you?'

'Given you're so determined to leave, I guess I'm not that good.' He tempered the words with that charming smile.

She paused by her open driver door and met the look in his delicious eyes. 'Right now I don't have any regrets. I stay and I might get them. I don't want to have any.'

'What about what I want? What about my regrets?'

'I can only apologise. Again.'

He walked closer, taking hold of the door. 'Never feel you have to apologise to me. Never ever.'

Unable to answer that, she got in the car. She'd not been honest about her lack of regrets. She regretted nothing of what had happened, but of what else could have happened had they been different people with desires that converged.

He closed the door for her but remained right by the car, expectantly. She fired the engine and hit the button to wind the window all the way down. He bent and leaned in so his face was right near hers.

'You don't get away that easy,' he murmured, sliding his hand to her jaw.

She couldn't accelerate away or she'd take his arm—

and head—with her. But there was no mistaking his intention.

The smile said it all and those gorgeously curved lips arrowed in on hers. The touch was firm—but not totally dominant as she'd expected. No, he held back for all of a second or two. But then his hand cupped her head, angling her slightly better to meet his as his lips plundered hers. And in another instant she plundered right back, seeking more of that strong touch, that deliciousness—the full impact of his utter masculinity. The shivers skittered down her spine, the knots coiled tighter and tighter in her belly already. His tongue swept—playful, insistent, driving. How could so much be said with a kiss?

She had no idea why she was gripping the steering wheel so tightly, or why she had her foot pushed so hard on the brake. The car engine wasn't even running. But she just knew she was in danger.

He stepped back. Her gaze was glued to him—to the fit, taut body and the smile that held as much rue as it did tease now. His big eyes burned right through hers.

'*My* regret...' he nodded slowly '...was not kissing you. Of course *now* I regret not kissing you sooner.'

Breathless, she put her hand on his wrist, seeking one last touch of skin. 'Thank you for being so nice to me.'

His gaze narrowed. 'I'm not as nice as all that, Ellie.' His voice dropped so she leaned forward in her seat, nearer to hear him. 'You need to know something about me.'

She waited, lungs not breathing, heart not beating.

'I'm man enough to take no for an answer,' he said. 'But I'm also man enough to fight for what I want.'

Eyes not blinking, she had to ask. 'What do you want?'

'You again. Every way. Any way.'

Oh.

He broke the drilling intensity with one of those shattering smiles that gave him such an unfair advantage. 'So if you want to go, you'd better go now.'

CHAPTER FOUR

'AND now, people, the moment you have been wait-ing for!' Despite the pelting rain, Ellie smiled, hugely enjoying the moment as she stepped aside to let them enter the cave—scene of the villain's final destruction.

The crowd cheered and walked in, a cacophony of excitement.

Four and a half unnaturally long weeks had passed. But the days were getting quicker—sure they were. Being super busy at work helped. She'd progressed from the day and overnight tours, to the longer three to seven nights. This was good, because being responsible for the well-being of up to a dozen people twenty-four hours a day meant she had little time to dwell on what might have happened had she not gunned the car and gone from zero to ninety in less than three seconds.

'OMG this is amazing!'

'I can't believe I'm actually here.'

'*Xaynethe*—at last!'

Ellie grinned as she took photos, photos and, oh, yes, more photos for the tourists as they posed outra-geously in front of the mother of all rocks that had been used in the penultimate scene of the mock-Greek-myth movie franchise.

Yeah, she too was the kind of girl who'd want to

dance in the *Sound of Music* summerhouse if she ever got to Salzburg. She'd go to Tiffany's and eat breakfast with her nose pressed to the window pane...so she totally got where her attendees were coming from. And she wanted them to have that experience of their lifetimes, for it to be worth the massive journeys they'd taken. They were die-hard fans, and die-hard fans did not like to be disappointed.

'Okay, random dialogue time—spot prize to the person who answers this.' She broke into a speech, one of the less famous quotes that eventually led into one of the film's greatest scenes.

One guy stepped up immediately, answering her bit-part player's throwaway comment with the hero's 'impassioned plea'. She continued the scene—taking another character's part, wanting to see how far he'd go and whether he could achieve UFS—Ultimate Fan Status. She set the bar super high so not many did, but she had a good feeling about this guy.

As she'd suspected, her tour 'hero' kept the exchange up for the entire scene—and when it ended, the rest of the group clapped and whistled. Laughing, Ellie took his hand and guided him to take a bow. Yeah, it really was the best job ever.

She checked her watch to ensure they weren't getting behind schedule. The movie re-enactment had gone on longer than she'd expected when he'd made it to UFS. 'Okay, everyone, you've got another fifteen here. I'll be at the bus finding Kenny's prize.'

Back outside the rain had eased—slightly. She bent her head, getting ready for the dash across the car park.

'You can't tell me you don't want to be an actress.' A drawl, right in her ear. 'Diva.'

She jumped, dropping her clipboard as she clutched

her chest—stopping her heart from literally leaping out of it.

'*Ruben,*' she puffed as she turned. 'You're here be-cause...?'

He handed her the clipboard he'd already retrieved. 'I was visiting the cave. Lucky coincidence, huh?'

Ellie wasn't convinced—not when his eyes twin-kled like that.

'You're amazing,' he continued, ignoring her as-tounded snuffle. 'You have them eating out of your hand. They're loving it. Even in the sodding rain they're loving it.'

He'd been watching them in there? Oh, that wasn't embarrassing at all.

'It's not me.' She rushed to snuff that burn in his eyes—and douse the roaring inferno that had com-busted in her belly at the mere sight of him. 'It's be-cause they're such fans of the film. Doesn't matter what I do, they're still going to be blown away by being here.'

He shook his head. 'No, you do everything for them and more. No small hassle too much trouble. Your pa-tience with the camera posing is phenomenal.'

He'd been watching a while, then? She giggled—and immediately cringed at her girlishness. 'I'm grit-ting my teeth over some of it. There are always one or two more difficult clients.'

'And one or two desperate to get into your pants.'

'Oh, that's not true.' But she blushed.

'That guy Kenny was all over you.'

'He was acting the part.' And she hadn't let him end that scene with the kiss that had happened in the movie.

'No, you're his leading lady now,' Ruben teased, stepping nearer. 'He's over his comic-book-heroine crush and fixed on someone real for the first time in his life.'

'He's just being friendly.'

'He's just being unsubtle.'

'And you're not?' She raised her brows at the way he'd moved in on her while speaking.

'Naturally I'm being as unsubtle as possible to let him and the rest of them know that you're not available.'

She glanced over his shoulder, panicking that some of her charges might come out of the cave and see her standing unprofessionally close to a random stranger. 'But I'm not available for you either.' A breathless rush of determined denial.

'I'm conveniently forgetting that for this moment.'

Hadn't she known he'd be difficult to handle? Totally the kind to tumble a girl to her back, and have her breathless and delighted before she'd so much as blinked. 'This isn't a good time,' she began.

'It's a perfect time. You have fifteen minutes before you have to round them back up on the bus.' He took her hand and led her across the car park, to the shelter of the trees on the far side. Out of anyone's view. 'Fifteen minutes…'

'Ruben…' Oh, this was not a good idea, but her heart was skipping and her limbs already sliding towards that warm, supple state. She inhaled deeply and valiantly strove for sanity. She was at *work*.

'Have you got any idea how gorgeous you look?' He sounded as if he wanted to eat her.

She needed to get a grip on both of them. 'I think you need to get to an optometrist—your vision appears to have gone soft-focus.'

He chuckled. 'Oh, no, I'm seeing very, very clearly.

In fact, I've got X-ray vision. I can see the lacy knickers even now.' He sighed. 'Lacy knickers under denim jeans.'

She couldn't help smile back at the sound of his laughter and the sight of his gorgeous—outrageous—face. So enticing. And exciting. Yeah, the rough denim was working its thing on her sensitive bits right about now.

'They are lacy, right?' he muttered in her ear as he swept her into his arms.

'What are you doing?'

'What do you think?' He laughed. 'I've wanted another kiss for weeks.'

She shook her head as she gazed up at him. She couldn't be so reckless again—certainly not now. 'You can't kiss me, you'll kill my lipstick.'

'It's alive?' One eyebrow up.

'It's neat and tidy and I don't want it all over my chin. I have to look good for them.'

His eyes narrowed. 'You look more than good. That Scottish sci-fi geek couldn't take his eyes off you.'

'It's the collectors' edition tee shirt—he wants it.'

'He wants what's in it. But he can't have it. I want it more.' His hands ran down her sides and it was all she could do not to melt into him.

Heaven help her, she was being turned on by macho possessive talk. 'I'm not an "it" and I'm at work.'

He nodded slowly and took a step back, his hands a feathering motion over her stomach as he stepped away. Too intimate and yet not enough. Damn. Her body screamed go-ahead-get-on-me. She didn't let that out; instead she strapped on a polite, *finite*, response. Because this guy would bring nothing but bad-boy trouble.

'I'd better get back to the bus, but thanks for stopping to say hi. It was nice to see you.'

His grin broadened, not seeming to take in her re-buff at all. 'Likewise.'

Ruben felt ridiculously pleased with himself for having tracked her down. It had taken less than five minutes in an online search. He'd hatched a cunning plan within another five. So now phase one was complete. Yes, hav-ing seen the bloom on her cheeks and the sparkle zing in her eye, he knew phases two and three were going to go so smoothly. He had the green light. An outsize amount of relief surged at her unguarded response because he was desperately—stupidly—hot for her. It wasn't as if he hadn't ever had a one-night stand before. He'd in-dulged in many a night of mutual thrills and minimal complexity. Just a 'hi' and a recognition of heat—that chemistry that guaranteed each would get their physi-cal kicks. Enjoyable. Ultimately forgettable.

But Ellie Summers had not been forgettable. It wasn't even the sex that he remembered most—although he was getting off on some seriously good slow-mo mental replays. It was her priceless reaction the next day—the earnest apologies and then the gorgeous giggles. Yeah, that brave ability to see the funny side and parry his shameless flirt with a tart, bald humour. And dignity. He hadn't been sure if she was cut up by that Nathan guy or not. He suspected not, but he'd decided to give her space to lick her wounds anyway. And he'd expected his usual once-done, all-done attitude would kick in.

It hadn't. So that was why he was leaning against his car, not caring about the rain, watching her tour bus slowly move out of the cave's car park.

* * *

At 9:00 a.m. the next day Ellie was in the office, wearing more make-up than usual to cover the effects of her
lack of sleep due to an embarrassing amount of Ruben
obsessing. But two minutes later, natural effervescence
had brought a smile to her face. 'I'm so pleased for you!'
she squealed at her beaming boss.

'I'm pleased for me too! And I want to thank you
so much.'

'It has nothing to do with me.' Ellie shook her head.
The full-colour, double-page magazine spread featur-
ing the popular movie-site tour company definitely had
nothing to do with her given she'd only been on the pay-
roll the last four weeks.

'Oh, yes, it has,' Bridie squealed back at her. 'You've
already got a name as the best guide *evah*—did you
know that group of German lads set up a Facebook page
as a tribute to the tour? Although the page is mainly
about you—they put your picture all over it.'

'They didn't.' Ellie gaped and embarrassment burned
her skin from the inside out.

'Uh-huh. It's a brilliant piece of word-of-mouth marketing.' Bridie tapped on her computer, bringing up the
website. 'Or pictures-of-tour-goddess marketing. Because as we know, a picture tells a thousand words. I put
a link to it on our website as one of the testimonials, as
well as liking it on our own Facebook page, of course.'

'You didn't.' Ellie winced at the picture of her mid-
spiel in front of the remains of the futuristic epic that
had been filmed a few kilometres up the road a few
years ago—the one that had been a massive hit in
Germany. They'd pinched the picture of her from the
official company website too, but at least in that one she
wasn't wearing a too-tight replica costume.

'Yes, and now we're fully booked for the next two

months and our Internet bookings are growing at a phenomenal rate and that's before this article came out.'
Bridie's smile faded. 'Although I suspect some of our
clients are going to be disappointed that it's not you
taking this tour this weekend.'

'I'm not taking the tour?' Surprised, Ellie turned
from the cringe-inducing page up on the computer.
She was all geared up for it—more than happy to work
weekends and extra shifts. It wasn't as if she had anything else to do. While she was the happiest she'd ever
been career-wise in her life, her personal life was dead
as a dodo—though she was happy about that too. She
was in restorative mode, building her new career, working on her personal issues. That left no room for a man.
And she refused, absolutely refused, to think about *him*.
Of course last night she'd absolutely failed on that front.
And the scenes her subconscious had chosen to replay
in her dreams—well, they'd been equally impossible
to control.

Now, for some reason, Bridie looked even more excited. 'No, because I'm sending you on a reconnais-
sance mission.'

'A what?'

Bridie looked about to burst. 'You know *Arche*?'

Of course she knew *Arche*. The multimillion-dollar
dystopian fantasy duo had been filmed almost exclu-
sively in New Zealand. It was one of her favourite film
series; she'd listed it first in her tour-guide bio on the
company website. There was one stop on her usual tour
that had a twenty-second scene in the second film; she
always stopped there and re-enacted it for the tourists.
Inevitably there was at least one *Arche*-freak on the bus
who loved it as much as she did.

'We might be granted access to it.' Bridie looked about to burst.

'What?' No one had been able to get into that set. The lower central South Island station where most of the action had been filmed was now one of those exclusive resort things for super-wealthy people. Some ancient South American rock star had opened it up for his equally famous and loaded buddies. Absolutely the kind of place she'd want to avoid—those kinds of exclusive retreat places made her think about not-so-distant mortifying events.

'They're thinking of allowing one tour operator in. And they want one of *our* reps to check it out.'

'And you want *me* to go?' Ellie gaped.

Bridie nodded furiously. 'By special request. They had a mystery shopper on all our tours and you're the guide who impressed them—so much so they want you to go check out the place and come up with some ideas for what you'd cover on a tour there.' Bridie jumped up from her seat and zipped around the office like a centipede on speed.

'But that's crazy,' Ellie screeched, collapsing into the nearest chair as her legs went woolly. 'I'm the newest recruit. You can't possibly trust me to do this.'

'It's not crazy. *You're* the one who knows those two films backwards—you can quote whole chunks of the dialogue, I heard you do it with one of those Brits the other day. You might be the newest recruit, but you're the best, most dedicated guide we've got.'

'But I can't represent you, I can't do the whole sales thing.' While she'd worked heaps on contracts at the location company, Ellie didn't have the experience to even think of it here.

'Don't worry about that. *I'll* be covering all access

and contract arrangements. All they're offering at the moment is the opportunity for you to tour the property and come up with the kind of spiel you'd do. They're concerned that as so much of the set was dismantled, there may not be enough there to build a tour around.'

Ellie rolled her eyes.

'I know.' Bridie chuckled near hysterically. 'Our film buffs would do anything just to see a blade of grass that might have been on screen. All you have to do is take a camera, think about the fans and we'll work on it when you get back.'

'You're not coming with me?' Ellie's hands went clammy with that mix of fear and excitement.

'It's the height of the season and our bookings have almost trebled. I'm taking your tour this weekend because you're the best asset to scope this new opportunity. And I'm trusting you with this because I don't want you head-hunted by another tour company and it's only a matter of time before they start calling you,' Bridie said, suddenly looking completely sober and intent. 'I know it's early days, but I know how much you love this and we both know how good you are. This is getting so big, so quick, I need someone like you heading it with me.'

Ellie had all but begged Bridie to give her this job when she'd hit the wall so hard at the location company. But it turned out it was the best thing she'd ever done because she loved it more than any other job—even the one where she'd got to fetch the twenty dollars a bottle water for that mega Hollywood star. It was hard work, but it was *fun*. And now? She couldn't believe she had this opportunity. 'Seriously?'

'Absolutely.' Bridie nodded, her smile returning.

'Okay, then, when am I going?'

Less than twenty-four hours later Ellie stepped off the plane at Queenstown airport dressed in her favourite-fitting jeans, white shirt, boots and her hair swished into a high ponytail. A man waited at the rail with her name scrawled on his board. He smiled and took her backpack.

'Ted Coulson, I'm driving you up there,' he introduced himself amiably. 'You'll need to save your questions for the boss, though. I only manage the deer farm business, not the lodge.'

'Okay.' She smiled, happy to feast her eyes on the amazing scenery for now anyway—the questions could come later. The snow-covered, spiky line of mountains was majestic and breathtaking. She could think of at least ten projects that had filmed in those Alps. She listed a few into her notebook and checked her watch to time the trip from airport to the station. But it wasn't too long before they left the main road and roared along a shingle one. Time disappeared as she breathed in the view—the mountains, the endless sky, the tussocky rolling land. Oh, yeah, no wonder the place was a popular choice for cinematographers—untouched beauty as far as the eye could see. Majestic.

But she blinked as the lodge came into view. 'Oh, wow.'

She knew there were several luxury properties around here, but this had to be one of the best. Man-made majesty this time.

'Something, isn't it?' Ted said dryly.

She breathed deep, trying to quell the nerves suddenly twanging just beneath her skin. 'It certainly is.' And she really, really didn't want to stuff this up.

Ted took the truck right up to the side of the house where there was a wide, covered porch, so passengers

could alight unruffled by inclement weather. He was
out of the car and opening her door before she'd managed to stop staring at the magnificence of the massive wooden door of the building. Yeah, just the door
had her amazed.

She stepped out of the car, feeling like a pixie who'd
mistakenly entered a giant's lair. She turned on the spot,
checking out the view the house had of the surrounding
mountains. This was out of her league. As Ted drove
away—apparently in a hurry to get back to his deer—
she heard that massive door swinging open and she
turned, her biggest smile switched on. She wanted to
make the best first impression ever.

Only her mouth gummed.

He had that 'Lucky' tee shirt on again. Those flattering blue jeans again. He had that smile again. The
same chocolate ganache eyes—glossy, deep brown.
And amused.

'Ellie Summers.' He held out his hand to shake hers,
that smile full on his face.

'*You* were the mystery shopper?'

He just grinned more.

'You watched like five minutes.'

'I saw all I needed to. It's obvious you have a gift.'

'Don't try to flatter me.'

'Why would I when I already know that won't work
with you? I'm merely stating a fact.'

She avoided looking him in the eye because she knew
if she did she was going to laugh and she refused to let
him away with it that easily. 'I'm not going to give you
what you want.'

'How do you know what I want?'

'I can see it in your eyes.'

'You're not looking at my eyes.'

She closed her own, knowing her skin was sizzling—aliens in outer space would be able to see the glow from her cheeks. She was both disappointed and excited—a zillion thoughts ran through her head in a nanosecond. This couldn't be his place—and if it was, had he brought her here under false pretences?

'You don't own this lodge,' she asserted. 'It belongs to an Argentinian guitarist.'

'Andreas sold it to my company last year and I truly do want to open it up for tours,' he said calmly, apparently able to read her mind.

'But you asked for *me*.' Not her boss or the other more experienced employees.

'Because you're the best guide. Inventive, best when you're improvising rather than sticking to a script someone else has written. So I want *you* to write the script. You're good at creating the fun scenarios.'

The fun scenarios? 'And that's all you want from me?' Now she was blushing more because she'd made a massive fool of herself in assuming...

'Oh, no,' he said as calmly as ever. 'I also want to have wild animal sex with you for hours until neither of us can move. But perhaps it isn't very politically correct of me to admit that.' A flash of that wide, wicked smile.

She choked. 'Not really.'

'Better to be honest though, isn't it?' Complete charm now.

'Um.' Speechless, she just stared at him. It was kind of flattering to think that the beneficiary of her one attempt at seduction had enjoyed it so much he wanted another. Except he'd probably be disappointed in any replay—why mess with the memory? And more importantly, she had her job to think of. 'You don't think mixing business with…this…is a bad idea?'

'I'm capable of not letting my personal life interfere with my professional.' He lifted his shoulders and let them drop easily. 'Are you?'

'Oh, you're just Mr Perfect, aren't you?'

'I'm glad you think so,' he muttered. 'Because I can definitely be perfect for you. I know exactly how I'm going to make you come.'

She moved, because a mere glance at him had her heating in places no one ought to know about. 'Why are you staring at me like that?' she croaked.

'I'm concerned,' he answered expressionlessly. 'You're feeling hot? You've gone very red.' He brushed her cheek with the backs of his fingers—a light caress that didn't just tease, it singed through her skin to her most elemental cell.

She lifted her chin and stepped back out of reach. 'Actually, I am feeling hot,' she answered honestly. 'You should probably keep your distance. One of the passengers on last week's tour came down with the flu. Trust me, if I'm getting that fever, you don't want it.'

'No.' His smile came, slow and wicked. 'I want it no matter what.'

'Ruben—'

'Don't worry.' He held up both hands. 'I shan't touch until you ask me to. And if you insist we'll never discuss it again. I just thought I'd let you know my plans for the weekend. You can let me know if yours dovetail with mine.'

'I'm here for the tour company, for my career and for no other reason.' Absolutely.

'Sure.'

Oh, the guy was too confident—and pretty much

had every reason to be. 'I'm not messing around with you again,' she asserted vehemently.

'Sure.' Too casually, he turned away from her. 'So let's get started.'

CHAPTER FIVE

Ellie followed Ruben inside—feeling like a pepper slow-burning over a bare flame. But while he might be all kinds of gorgeous, she was no longer Ms People-Pleaser Total Pushover. She'd drawn her line and she was holding it. She was here to work—and work was all that was important to her at the moment.

'You know the lodge wasn't used in the movies at all,' he said, leading her through the building, her overnight bag slung over his shoulder. 'So it won't be available for the tour. We're really just talking about those big hills and the remnants of the set buildings.'

'Okay, but they're going to need refreshments at some point. It's quite a hike to get here.' She was starving. The biscuit and coffee snack on the plane hadn't done much to fill her tummy's gap.

He nodded. 'There's a guest house further down the road. We can do morning tea or something. I have a cook.'

Of course he did.

'Actually, that cook has left something for us to eat tonight if you're hungry,' he said—still with that too-casual attitude.

She wished she had the reserves to say no but she knew it was in her best interests to get her blood sugar levels balanced or she'd be in danger of flying off yet another handle and doing something completely crazy. And merely watching his rear view fell into crazy category. Two minutes of following him had rendered her light-headed. The temptation to do *him* was lunatic.

'I'd love something to eat, thanks.' She'd think food, food, and nothing but food.

He turned, surprised at her easy acquiescence. 'Sooner rather than later?'

'Definitely.' She nodded enthusiastically. 'And I'd love a drink.'

He laughed, which really didn't help her battle to resist her attraction to him. 'No problem.' He led her to the massive, all-professional-equipped kitchen. 'There's a fantastic cellar here. Did you want red, white or bubbly?'

She rolled her eyes. 'Water straight from the tap will do me just fine, thanks.'

'You don't want any wine?' he asked in mock surprise. 'No French champagne tonight?'

'I'm not so stupid I'd make that mistake a second time,' she answered with spirit.

'You blame the bubbles?' He smiled.

She took the glass of chilled water he offered. 'No, but I don't think it helped. I'm grown-up enough to accept most of the madness was my own fault.'

He watched her from the other side of the granite-topped bench. 'What about the lodge—does the décor inspire you as much as the chateau's did?'

Ruefully she sipped, flushing her boiling system with the almost frozen water, and refused to answer. Instead she turned away from the gorgeously deluxe interior to look out of the window at the amazing skyline. 'How many of these places do you own?' She needed their addresses so she could avoid them at all costs. Just her luck that when she finally got to go somewhere gorgeous, her one most wicked encounter would have to be waiting.

'Last count it was five. I'm working on the sixth and seventh at the moment.'

'That's quite a stable.' Especially given each came with a multimillion-dollar price tag.

'They're not all as big as this one. But they keep me busy.'

She glanced back at him as he answered. Yes, there was the slightest hint of tiredness about his eyes. On the bench was the laptop, the tablet, the smart phones—all the paraphernalia of the businessman who worked 24/7.

'But the chateau was the first?' She pressed for more information. 'And it was your father who built it?' And who'd had the folly of the marriage?

'It had been his dream, but he got sick before he could finish it,' Ruben answered, no flicker of emotion crossing his face.

'Oh, I'm sorry.'

'Cancer.' He elaborated a fraction. 'He was older. It was only to be expected, I guess.'

'So you took it over?' She skimmed over his father's age reference for now. She was more interested in how on earth Ruben had managed to achieve all he had.

He nodded.

'How old were you?'

'Fourteen when he died, seventeen when I took on the chateau.'

'*Seventeen?*'

The roguish smile appeared at her amazed tone. 'My mother signed it over to me.'

'She did?'

He nodded as if it were completely everyday and then turned to the massive stainless-steel fridge. 'I wanted it, she didn't.'

Ellie was gobsmacked. Who on earth signed over a massive property to a teenager? 'Where's your mother now?'

'She went back to France a few months after he died. She didn't want to be hounded as a merry widow.'

'But you stayed?' All alone in New Zealand, barely old enough to leave school, let alone take on a massive business project?

'I wanted to finish the chateau.' He pulled a covered dish from the fridge and put it into the microwave, pressing the electronic controls, still speaking in that carefree way. 'I wanted to realise my father's dream. But Mama couldn't face it. I don't blame her for that.'

His mother had been that unhappy? And had their relationship been so fragmented she'd chosen to leave her only child behind? It seemed Ruben had some pain in common with Ellie's. 'Do you see her much?' Ellie couldn't resist asking and her curiosity didn't seem to bother him given the way he answered so easily.

'We use Skype and stuff but we're both busy. She has a small boutique she loves. I'm flat out,' he answered with that easy-going smile.

Okay, so maybe that relationship wasn't the greatest. But hadn't he had a better one with his dad? 'You must have been close to your father to want to finish his dream for him.'

Ruben's smile became fixed. 'He died a while back now.'

Yeah, but some wounds remained, never truly healing. While you got on with it, there was that permanent bruise beneath the skin. And though Ellie hadn't lost anyone close, she still understood heartbreak—in her case for what could have been, for what she'd missed out on from both parents. 'You don't have any other family?'

He shook his head. 'Nor do I want any.' He turned and caught her eye. His chocolate gaze held pointed meaning, despite the wicked seductiveness of his smile. 'I'm not a wedding-ring kind of guy.'

'Is that you trying to be subtle?' she asked, flipping to tart. 'You don't need to warn me. I'm not coming *anywhere* near you.'

'Oh, right.' He chuckled. 'My mistake.'

Arrogant sod. Of course, she couldn't help smiling and she couldn't help her curiosity. 'So, why no commitment? What's your marriage-avoidance excuse? You had a close shave with a stereotypically money-hungry woman or something?' She rolled her eyes at the cliché. Successful men always seemed to fear some big bad woman was going to come after half their assets in the divorce court or something.

'No.' He walked the few paces back to the business end of the kitchen, pulled a salad bowl from the fridge. 'It's a matter of priority. *Work* is my priority and has been for a while. It takes up every minute of every day and that's not about to change. I travel a lot between venues. I can't be at someone's beck and call.'

Beck and call? She frowned. 'We're talking marriage, not *servitude*.'

'There's a difference?' He smiled as if he was joking—kind of. 'I can't be anyone's husband. I can't be the guy who's going to be there for all those "important" things. It's not fair of me to promise that only to let someone down time after time. I don't want resentment to build and then be hurled against me.'

Was that what had happened? He'd been with someone who'd demanded too much of his time? But wouldn't a woman know what she was getting into in a relationship with a guy like him? That the career drive was an inseparable part of the man she'd fallen for? Just as a woman who married a military man would know that both she and he would have to sacrifice some things because of his duty? Didn't those relationships still work—*with* some work?

Yeah, maybe that was it. Maybe Ruben spent so much energy on his business, he couldn't be bothered working on sustaining a relationship. And why should he have to when he undoubtedly had billions of women throwing themselves at him?

'No, that's still just an excuse,' she said callously. 'You don't want to commit to a woman because you can get what you want from any number. Why would you limit yourself to just one?'

He filled a bowl from the rice cooker on the utility bench, grinning as he did so. And he didn't deny it. 'Let's eat.' He faced her with that smile. 'We'll feel better for it.'

'A microwave meal,' she gushed. 'I'm *so* excited.'

'Why don't you try it before casting judgment?'

Ellie met his challenge with a tilt of her chin and kept her chin high as he relentlessly watched her take first bite of the light curry.

'Okay, best microwave meal ever,' she mumbled, even though her mouth was still half full. There was no point trying to lie in the face of that piercing scrutiny.

He laughed softly and started in on it too.

Dinner passed too quickly because it was so damn delicious. She complimented his chef several times over—to his amusement. Conversation remained safe—

restaurants in Wellington, cafés on the wine trail. After, she helped him carry the dishes back to the bench, helped him rinse and stack them into the machine. And all that time she refused to let herself think on the fact that the guy was good company.

But he was. Really good company. And he was seducing her.

As that thought finally wriggled its way to the front of her brain she glanced at her watch. 'What time do we set out tomorrow?'

'After breakfast, which will be whenever you wake up. There's no real rush.'

'Well, I should probably—'

'Sit down on the sofa and look at the view,' he interrupted with that wolfish manner. 'It's nowhere near bedtime. We need to talk some more.'

'Don't you have work to do?' she asked, desperately aware she needed to get away from him. The longer she was in his presence, the more addled her brain became. It wasn't right that someone could exude such intoxicating heat. And now, as he walked her to the lounge with the amazing view and the sofas that were made for snuggling on, memories tormented, making her all the more susceptible.

'I always have work to do,' he answered carelessly. 'That's not the point.'

She took a seat, primly keeping her knees and ankles firmly together, avoiding looking at him. 'What did you want to talk about?'

'The movies,' he answered promptly, flopping onto the sofa opposite. 'Which of the two is your favourite?'

'*Seriously?*' She glanced at him. 'I wouldn't have thought you had much respect for movies. I'm guessing you don't have much *time* for them.'

'Not usually.' He blithely ignored her dig. 'But I made a point of watching them the other day and found they weren't bad. Talk me through the fandom.'

So she did. To her surprise, he really had watched them and remembered lots of detail. And had even enjoyed them. Then it turned out he'd watched a few classic films in his time. And a ton of French ones.

'Anything with Gérard Depardieu?' She giggled.

'Makes for a lot of movies.' He winked. 'My mother loves him and Dad used to try and impersonate him— badly.'

So there had been good times with his parents?

'How come you developed such a passion for the flicks?' he asked, switching the focus back on her.

'Oh, I just watched a lot as a kid. Habit.'

'Your parents liked them?'

No, she hadn't been curled up on a sofa between her parents watching a film as he probably had. She'd been in her own bedroom with her own telly—to her friends' envy—and watched them alone. She still had a massive DVD collection. 'They were just fun.'

A time-filler, a window into another, more friendly, world—where villains got their comeuppance, orphans found families and plain girls got the guys. Sure they might be fairy tales, but she enjoyed them.

'And you really like taking the tours?' he asked as if he couldn't understand why anybody would.

'Being with the fans is way more fun than working behind the scenes,' she explained. '*I'm* a fan—I understand that excitement. I mean, it's hard work, but I love it. And I love travelling. I love getting to meet these interesting people who've come from so far away. Who've been to other interesting places. Who love the movies I do. It's fantastic.'

The discussion was a timely reminder—she *wasn't* going to stuff up her perfect job by sleeping with one of the possible contacts. Again.

'I can see why you're popular. Your enthusiasm is infectious,' he said slowly, with a look in his eyes that she was sure wasn't good. 'You know there's a pool here,' he drawled.

Definitely not good. She had another melt moment and instantly rallied. 'I didn't bring my swimsuit. And don't even suggest skinny dipping.' Yeah, she'd caught the flicker of his smile.

'It's heated. There's a spa as well.'

She'd known staying to chat with him wouldn't be wise. She might be completely sober but she was suddenly as giddy as if she'd sucked a litre of champagne through a straw. 'I don't need to try all the things you have for your high-paying guests. I'll be with the scraggly film fans out in the muddy field.'

'I just thought it might help you relax.' He opened his hands in an oh-*so*-not innocent gesture.

'Let down my guard, you mean.' She wasn't here to relax.

'How about a ride, then?' He roared with laughter at her expression. Then clarified. 'We could just go along the fence-line, you could see the moon and the stars. Very much a movie scene.'

'I'm not really into horse-riding.' And she refused to blush. 'We have all day tomorrow to see the old set. I think it's best if I turn in for an early night.'

'You're afraid.'

'Of horses, yes.' She dared him to laugh at her. 'And I'm being sensible.'

He let out a theatrical sigh. 'Come on, then, Cinderella.' He scooped her bag from where they'd left it in the kitchen and then led her up the stairs—another wide, plush corridor that seemed to go for ever.

'Now.' He opened a door and put her bag just inside. 'This is your bedroom.'

'Thank you.' She walked into the room and quickly turned, her hand closing the door. But before she could slam it in his face he leaned in.

'Pay very close attention,' he drawled. 'My bedroom is a mere three doors along. Same floor and everything. You can't miss it. Even if there's a power cut and it's pitch black. Worst case just try them all, there's no one else staying here, only me to be found.'

'Dream on.'

'Oh, I do. Every night.' He shrugged, utterly unashamed. 'Just as you do.'

'There's a lock on this door, isn't there?' She looked down at it as if to ensure it.

'There's no full moon tonight,' he continued, ignoring her interruption. 'Just as there wasn't then. You don't need to pretend you're a horny were-woman, just do what you want to do.'

'*You're* not what I want to do,' she muttered, determined to believe it.

'I think I prefer it when you're agitated and honest rather than trying to be cool and lie.'

She choked—torn between laughter and outrage. 'You're so up yourself.'

'No, I'm just not so uptight I can't admit to something that feels good.'

She twitched. 'Look, what happened was a mistake. I'm all for learning from my mistakes.'

'Well, frankly, I'm glad you made the wrong room mistake and saved yourself from a mess-up with that other guy.'

'What happened with you was a mistake too.'

'How can you say that?' His voice dropped lower still. A whisper that slid over her like the faintest, warmest of breezes. 'You're as in thrall as I am.'

She had to end this somehow, before she went up in a puff of smoke. 'This is really flattering and all—' she sucked up some cool '—but I'm not available for anyone, or any kind of thing, right now. That night just showed what an idiot I was.'

'You weren't an idiot.' He looked concerned. 'That wasn't the act of a desperate woman.'

'Wasn't it?' Wasn't it exactly that?

It was one of the few moments in the evening where his expression was serious. 'There's nothing wrong with having needs and giving them free expression. You know what I think of you?' he asked.

She really didn't want to know.

'That you're a spontaneous, fiery, passionate woman who's as human as I am. Who makes mistakes, who has wants. It was refreshing. You were in total charge. You blew my—'

'Look, don't try to make out like I'm some kind of sex goddess just because you want back in my pants.' Ellie breathed in desperately. 'Truth is I don't want any kind of a relationship right now. I've got a new job that I really don't want to lose because I actually love it. I want to be in charge of both my career and my social life.'

'I don't want a relationship either.' His shoulders lifted. 'It's impossible for me. I'm in the middle of a new deal, I'm away every week to another hotel.' He half laughed. 'And that's not going to change any time soon. And not for anyone.'

'So there's really nothing to talk about, right?'

'There is just this one small thing.' He leaned closer.

'You said you wouldn't make a move.'

'I'm not.'

'You know you are.' She shook her head. 'Why don't you drive to the nearest bar or something? You could get sex any time you want it.'

'You're proving that statement wrong right this second.'

She swallowed.

'I have some fun when it feels right, but my field's been empty a while.' He maintained his intent, fiery gaze on her. 'I can admit to my needs, maybe you can't. But your actions that night showed you have them.'

'It can't happen.'

'Yes, it can. Just once more can absolutely happen.'

Just once more. Oh, so, so tempting.

'You promised you wouldn't touch me unless I invited it.' Her whisper was invitation enough and they both knew it.

She looked down to stop the mesmerising effect of his easy smile and dangerous eyes. But it merely made it worse because now she could *hear* the molten-chocolate quality in his words. She could feel his heat; her own instinct to draw nearer pulled.

'Look at me.' Now there was more than a thread of steely persuasion in that warm voice.

She fought the urge to obey—because he wasn't going to win her around. She wasn't going to roll over like so much of her *wanted* to.

He braced his hands in the door frame and leaned across the threshold.

And she felt it, she really did. His proximity was as good as a touch, spiking her adrenalin, sending shivers along her skin despite that inch of air between his body and hers.

'Ruben,' she barely breathed.

She could retreat into her room but she didn't want to back down in any kind of way. Besides, he'd simply follow her in and that would decimate her control.

'I'm not touching you,' he murmured, his sensual dominance merciless. 'Do you want me to?'

He didn't have to touch her to tempt her. But his incredible magnetism equally repelled her. More games with him would inevitably cause hurt for her—she always ended up the heartbroken, not the heartbreaker. She'd had only that one night of playing carefree seductress, whereas he'd had many as seducer. And worse, more games could cost her future with the best job she'd ever had. So despite the desire threatening to enslave her, she couldn't succumb to it.

'Good night.' She shoved him back through the doorway and quickly shut the door.

A split second of silence and then he called a teasing comment through the wood. 'Enjoy those dreams, darling.'

Oh, she would, but dreams were all they were going to be.

CHAPTER SIX

'It's supposed to be summer.' Stupidly forlorn, Ellie stared out of the window at the grey-blanketed land. The steady drizzle had drenched all her plans for the day. How were they going to get out and see the set remnants in this? How was she going to get through another hour under the same roof as Ruben and not jump him— even a roof as huge as this? She *had* to get out of there.

'It's not so bad.'

She turned. He was jeans-clad again. And it was worse than bad.

'Come and eat something.' He took her trembling for hunger of the food kind.

'We can still ride if you don't mind getting wet,' he commented, not quite idly, once she'd filled her cereal bowl.

Okay, maybe he knew exactly how much his mere presence tormented her. But she wasn't ever admitting how wet she already was.

'I'm not riding with you.' She glared at him, her spoon halfway to her mouth. She was a frustrated wreck who hadn't managed to get nearly enough sleep and infuriated with her inability to restrain her attraction to him.

'If you won't go on a horse, then it's the quad bike.

It's too far to walk and it's rough country, especially in this weather.' He shrugged. 'But lots of your tourists would like quad biking, right?'

Quad biking would mean her straddling the seat behind him, her arms around his waist. He was determined to breach her personal space again, wasn't he? And she was melting already. She shoved the loaded spoon into her mouth and chomped.

'I can ride one myself,' she declared once she'd swallowed. She was not cuddling him from behind.

'Of course.' He acted as if there'd been no other option anyway. 'Finish your breakfast. I'll go get the bikes ready.'

She was glad to see him go—truly glad: his back view didn't ever worsen any. Not with the casual jeans and clinging tee and, oh, so confident way he had of walking.

So he can walk—she winced at her fan-girly brainlessness—*many men can*. She returned her focus to the cereal and consumed the lot. If one type of hunger wasn't going to be sated, another would. At least her legs would lose the cotton-wool feeling.

But twenty minutes later she was astride a powerful machine, with her thighs vibrating. She'd never stand again at this rate. Oh, it was not good. She could *not* be getting turned on by a hulking great piece of metal. Of course she wasn't, she was *already* on.

'Which way?' she shouted breathlessly as he paused for her to come alongside his bike.

He just jerked his thumb in answer.

For almost an hour and a half they rode, stopping lots as he pointed out where filming had occurred. Then they powered out and let the machines roar. And she loved every damn second of it. Even in the drizzly,

greyed-out day, the landscape was so majestic and ancient, it put all those pesky little things like unquenched
lust into perspective—blowing away the sleepless bad
temper and leaving exhilaration in its wake.

He, too, had the red-cheeked, bright-eyed excitement.
'Come on, we can go further up the valley.'

'The weather doesn't worry you?'

'No, are you okay?'

'I'm good.' Whether the scenery had been another
character in a globally massive movie franchise or not,
it was simply stunning. And she wanted more of this
wild open air—with him. No matter that her jeans were
mud splattered, that the drizzle had gone right through
the light coat she was wearing over her jeans so her
tee shirt was soaking. As the rain tumbled faster and
heavier she was steaming up inside.

She followed his lead across the short tussocky track,
down to the vast shingle riverbed. They were about two
miles along that when the rain really began to fall. Their
wheels churned up large globs of mud. She blinked rap-
idly to maintain clear vision but ahead of her Ruben's
engine roared angrily as he pushed it. His bike jerked
forward and Ellie winced, barely able to watch through
half-screwed lids. Despite knowing what was about to
happen, she was unable to do anything to help except
shout. But even as she did Ruben jumped. His machine
tipped, two wheels disappearing into a muddy bank. A
half second later, Ruben rolled to his feet in total stunt-
man style.

'Hello, Mud-man,' she teased, hiding the relief that
he wasn't injured. Thankfully they hadn't been going
fast enough for a serious accident.

He was laughing, his eyes alight as he yanked off his

helmet and surveyed the damage. 'I'm going to need a truck to get the bike out of there.'

Ellie refused to notice how his hair had spiked in places, making him look more of a carefree rogue than ever. She hated to think what her own hair looked like now she'd removed her helmet too. More horrendous was the fact they were stuck miles from the lodge and had to share the one bike to get back.

'You did this deliberately, didn't you?' she accused, her adrenalin finding a vent in anger.

'I'm capable of many great things, but controlling the weather isn't one of them.' His laughter became more rueful. 'This part was more boggy than I expected. And if you must know, the rain bothers me more than it does you.'

'And why's that?' She didn't believe him.

'I had plans for today.'

Still astride her bike, she put her hands on her hips. 'Nefarious ones?'

'Utterly,' he admitted shamelessly. 'Now they're ruined.'

'So what are you going to do about it?'

'Oh, I always have a Plan B.' He chuckled.

Yeah, the guy was so confident in his ability to turn even the worst situation to something favourable. His plan involved charming the pants off her, no doubt. But while he was incredibly focused in his attention on her, somehow he made it impossible to get past *his* front. It wasn't that he wasn't genuine—unlike Nathan, she knew Ruben was honest in his desire to be with her. But while he answered her questions, he wouldn't let her past a certain point in his reserve. He closed conversation down or switched focus. But Ellie was both curious and determined not to let him have it all his own way.

'Don't think I'm handing over my bike to you,' she said, remaining firmly astride her vehicle. 'You're too reckless.'

He walked right in her path, leaning forward to put his hands over hers on the handlebars. 'You're going to make me walk back?'

'I'll drive, you give directions.'

'You do like to be in control of the situation, don't you?' he muttered.

In less than ten seconds she knew she'd made a mistake. He'd come round and climbed behind her and was now way too close with his hands too firm around her waist. If she'd been the one to take the rear position she could have made it less intimate.

'You don't have to hold so tight, you know,' she said firmly. 'I'm not going to drive that fast.'

All she felt then was the laughter vibrating in his chest. She wanted to lean back and absorb it some more. Instead, she put the engine on full throttle.

'Wow, you really know what you're doing,' he commented after she rode them out of the roughest part of the riverbed at high speed. 'You could go on one of those extreme environment survivor shows. Wild Mountain Woman or something.'

'Don't get too carried away.' She slowed down to hear him better. 'It's not like I'm going to rappel down a rock face using a rope I've plaited out of dental floss,' she scoffed. 'I know my own limitations.'

'Really? What's your limit?'

She ignored the innuendo and answered honestly. 'I still get a bit scared of heights.'

'Still?'

'I get a bit funny in the tummy but most of the time I can manage to control it.' She eased back more as she came to a badly bogged bit. 'My dad is really into rock-climbing and mountaineering and stuff. He'd be in his element here.'

'You go climbing with him?'

'When I was younger I did,' she said briefly. 'If I wanted to spend time with him, he was usually somewhere precarious so I had to suck it up.'

'And you wanted to spend time with him?'

'Sure.' He was her dad. All her life she'd wanted his attention and approval—until she'd grown up enough to accept it wasn't ever going to be forthcoming. 'I've never really understood his need to conquer nature, though. I mean, yes, appreciate the beauty, respect the elements, come and enjoy it. But why does he have to *beat* it? Where's the rush in risking life and limb? Man versus nature? Nature is always going to win.'

'Hmm.' Ruben grunted a kind of agreement. 'Where does he live?'

'He has an outdoor equipment store in one of those ski towns not too far up the road from here.'

'Oh.' A pause. 'Did you want to see him while you're down here?'

'No.'

Another slight pause. 'What about your mum? She's into the outdoors too?'

'No, she's the total opposite. While Dad's all mountain man, she's city-queen. She lives in Sydney.'

'They're divorced?'

'Have been for nearly twenty years.'

She heard his whistle. 'How'd they manage to meet and marry in the first place?'

'They were a fling, she got pregnant. They tried to make it work but, really, it was never going to. It would have been easier if they'd ended it sooner.'

'But they wanted you,' he said, as if that made it all okay.

Sometimes she thought it would have been better if they'd adopted her out to a couple who'd been desperate to have kids. Yes, she was grateful to them for making the decision to have her, but to raise her themselves? They were too selfish for that. Neither had wanted to give up the things important to them. Ellie had had to fit in—to tag along. But she'd never felt truly wanted, never once felt as if she could make them happy. Just once, just for once, she wanted to be the centre of the universe. Not to have to try to squeeze herself into some contortion to fit into the box of someone else's life. Every kid wanted her parents' undivided attention and love. No kid could ever have enough—especially if they'd been starved of it.

'They did the shared-custody thing, but that was be-cause neither wanted me full time.'

His grip on her waist tightened as he pressed in even closer. 'What do you mean neither wanted you full time?'

'I mean exactly that.' Ellie hesitated—did she really want to go into this? Nothing put a guy off more than a woman who went on about her exes or unhappy home life. Men hated drama. And Ruben had already declared he wasn't into the whole 'being there' deal. Given that, it was probably *wise* to talk about it. Tell him all the crap to turn his interest off and shore up her own resis-tance. So she slowed more so he could hear her easily.

'You know, week about? One week with Mum, one week with Dad,' she explained. 'Everybody thinks it's great. You get double of everything. Different rules, different homes. Supposedly you can get away with stuff because you say the other parent "would let you".

But for me it wasn't like that. I wouldn't have minded a few more rules—at least then it might have felt like they cared.'

Some spats between them, some arguments over her welfare might have made things seem more normal. But the arguments had been because both her parents preferred their child-*free* week. The week they had scheduled with her was the one that hindered them. She'd heard the whispered fury when one had tried to get out of a weekend or a week of responsibility. The annoyance of having to have her—that her presence meant ruined plans. They'd each wanted their time *away* from her so badly. So instead of doing what *she* wanted, she'd tried so hard to do whatever it was that they wanted to do. To blend, to be good, to please. The only thing that had been easy was the actual move. Trying to fit into each destination was the exhausting bit. In the end she'd just kept quiet in her room, watching her favourite movies. And when old enough, hanging with some girlfriends, and then finding attention in the arms of guys who wanted what she had to offer, but didn't want to give what she needed.

'You're their only child?' he asked.

'Yeah, that's a good thing given the way they were. But it would have been nice for me to have had company.'

'So what, you have some Waltons family dream now?' he teased.

She laughed. 'I'm realistic enough to know that's a fantasy.'

'Hell, yes,' he said with feeling.

'How do you know it is a fantasy?' she couldn't resist challenging. 'You're an only child too.'

'But I grew up down the road from a number of

Waltons-esque families. And let me tell you, they were superficial images. I think it's better off staying small. *Very* small.' As in solitary. But even though he knew the answer, even though he knew this was a hopeless conversation, Ruben couldn't resist asking her, 'Are you into kids?'

'I'm not sure. Probably not.'

'Really?' Most girls didn't mean it when they went all definite denial. But Ellie hadn't been definite; she seemed more thoughtful.

'Not unless I meet the right guy, you know?' she finally expanded. 'He really has to be the *right* guy. I need him to be there and I need him to want the kid. It's not nice not to be wanted. I want any kids of mine to have two parents who want them, who love them, who are there for them. For everything.'

Ruben understood—she wanted her kids to have the kind of parents she *hadn't* had. He felt hurt for her, but impressed at the same time with her courage. Now she knew what she wanted and she wasn't going to settle for less. Not for some guy like *him*. Because he already knew he couldn't 'be' there. His one significant ex had wanted him to 'be' there—and that was just for her, not kids as well. If he couldn't be there enough for a grown woman, there was no way he could be there for children.

'I'm guessing you're a no-kids man?' Ellie sounded amused at his silence.

'I like kids but they wouldn't fit in my life. I'm not someone who can guarantee to "be there" for them. I've got things I want to do and I don't think it's fair to have a family when you can't give them everything they want.'

'That beck-and-call thing, huh?' she asked dryly.

She might be all sarcasm, but he meant it. He didn't

want a family holding him back from all he could achieve. He didn't have the ability or the desire to meet the demands of a long-term relationship. He'd tried it years ago with Sarah and failed miserably. And his father had succeeded in the relationship but failed on the business front. There was no such thing as managing it all. 'I'm years off being ready for it in terms of my career and I don't want to be old like my father was. I love him for having me, but I wish he'd done it sooner.'

'So your mum was quite a bit younger?'

'Try thirty years,' he admitted shortly. 'Hard to have everyone thinking he was your grandfather.' He chuckled to lighten it the way he always did. 'And the looks the two of them got when they were walking along the street, hand in hand and smooching like teen lovers. They just didn't give a damn.'

He felt her stiffen beneath his fingers and felt the old resentment burn in his gut. He hated intolerance.

'I thought they had an unhappy marriage?' Ellie had all but stopped the machine. 'Isn't that what you meant by his folly of a marriage?'

'Oh, no.' Ruben laughed, relieved her tension hadn't been in judgment of his parents. 'No, people couldn't cope with their age gap.'

'And gave you a rough time over it?'

'You can imagine the slurs at a small-town school back then.'

'What's wrong with two people making each other happy?' Ellie sounded as if she was frowning. 'Why can't people just be pleased for them? Doesn't everyone want to find a great love like that?'

He smiled at her naïveté—she'd watched too many Hollywood happy endings. 'People can be unkind when they don't understand or if it's something they've not been around much.' He hardly ever discussed it, he'd encountered too much intolerance—even in this supposedly modern world. There was just that inevitable smirk or comment—as if his dad were up there with Hugh Hefner or something. But Ellie's instant emo defence of them had him explaining more than he usually would. 'They really were a love match and really in love. Sickening really.' Sometimes even he'd felt excluded from it. This despite knowing he'd been the much-wanted, much-loved product of their relationship. And he'd been determined not to break their blissful ignorance and had never once told them of the taunts he'd suffered. He'd learned to handle the other kids his own way. When he'd first started school as an undersized six-year-old, with English as a second language, a weird accent in a small town with a father already almost at retirement age and a mother younger and more beautiful than everyone else's? It had been sink or swim—and Ruben had mastered the stroke. 'They just saw through each other's layers to the person within, and they loved what they saw.' He still felt that mix of happiness for them and frustration with them—because they'd been unable to achieve much else because of that total adoration of each other.

'Has your mum met anyone else since?' Ellie asked quietly.

'No. I kind of wish she would,' he found himself admitting aloud for the first time in his life. 'But she's adamant it isn't going to happen.'

'Because she buried her heart with him?'

'Yeah. I think she's scared of getting that hurt again.' He understood that too. The loss had been unbearable. 'She couldn't stay in New Zealand. Couldn't stay any place where she'd been with him.'

'But what about you? You were so young.' Ellie's body had gone taut beneath his fingertips again.

He laughed off her concern—the way he laughed off anything that touched too close to vulnerable aches. 'I wanted to finish what he'd started. I wanted to do that for him.'

'But it must have hurt her to leave you?'

Her sweet concern stabbed now and he didn't want it. 'Mama knew I was okay. And I was busy.' He'd made sure she'd thought he was okay. By then he was a master of hiding his hurt—those years of coping with childhood taunts had taught him well. You covered up—no one could grin and bear it like Ruben. He could turn any nightmare around with a comment and a smile, hiding how gutted he might be inside. He'd won them over with the ability to laugh and make others laugh—but he never let them close. Not when he knew too well how much it hurt to lose those you held close.

'It would have hurt her more to stay.' He dismissed the topic completely, switching to tell her something more about the mountain on their right, and then another anecdote from when Andreas had owned the lodge.

As the big building came into view he directed her to take the bike right up to the main entrance. He'd have it cleaned and put away later. For now it was the two of them who needed hosing down. Indeed, off the bike the first thing Ellie did was glower at his mud-covered clothes and then down at her own.

'I don't have any other jeans, you realise.'

Ruben couldn't contain his amusement. She looked like an earth goddess—a curvy sprite of a woman. Little curls had sprung around her temples, her face damp, her eyes shining. 'You can borrow some of mine.'

'Like they'd fit.'

'They'll be fine. Now come on, I'm freezing,' he lied. 'We don't want to get a chill.'

He'd taken the cover off the spa pool early this morning and he headed straight for it.

'I told you I didn't bring my swimsuit.' She followed him round the side of the lodge and stared at the pool with an unmistakably longing gleam in her eye.

Yeah, Ellie had a sensualist streak—he wanted her to embrace it.

'I'll give you a shirt that'll do.' She was going to have to peel off those blue jeans. He'd never appreciated denim as much before and he was a jeans-every-day guy. But hers were wet, hugging her curvy butt and thighs and he wanted to slide his hand down the tight front of them really badly.

He went into the pool house and grabbed a tee, tossing it at her and exiting before he turned into some kind of caveman and went for her mud and all.

He stripped poolside while she was in the change room, and forced himself to go under the outdoor shower—cold—sluicing away the streaks of dirt before quickly getting into the heated water. He badly needed to relax.

'You can't resist it, can you?' she teased as she came out of the pool house, ready to join him. She too had showered. Now his clean shirt was clinging to her wet body beneath.

Ruben pressed the spa bubbles on full to hide how horrifically extreme her effect on him was.

'Resist what?' he asked vaguely. Thinking about sex all the time? Hell, he wished he could get her out of his head, or at least get some other woman in. He'd never been unhealthily fixated on one lover like this.

He blamed it on the absolute excitement of waking to discover a hot, perfect lover straddling him. Pure fantasy come to life.

Of course he couldn't help thinking of it and nothing but. Of course he'd had to finagle a way of getting her back in his bed—even just for a weekend. Only it wasn't proving to be as simple as he'd planned.

'Seeking out pleasure.' She shook her head, shivering as she stepped carefully into the steaming water.

'I work hard so why shouldn't I enjoy playtime?' He sent her a sideways look and jeered lightly. 'Nothing wrong with relaxing and celebrating and enjoying pleasure. We should appreciate it when something feels good.'

'Don't think you can get me to yes by glamorising hedonism,' she answered equally flippantly.

'But you know how good it was. You *told* me how good it was.' And he'd loved hearing it. 'The best ever.' And he couldn't get past it now, not when she was doing the wet-tee-shirt thing in a hot tub.

'It's bad form to compare lovers,' Ellie said primly, sitting on the opposite side of the spa from him and determinedly not looking at his bare chest. She didn't believe for a second that he actually felt the same way— *she* hadn't been his best lover ever as well.

'I'm not doing that.' He laughed. 'I'm merely reminding you that that night with me was the best sex of your life. I can't understand why you don't want a repeat of that.'

'Because it wasn't real,' she said simply.

'It wasn't real?' Ruben's tease vaporised. 'Wasn't *real*?'

In a heartbeat the relaxed, teasing atmosphere

snapped to stormy. Ellie's suddenly feverish temperature couldn't be blamed on the bubbling water.

'No, it wasn't real,' she insisted.

He stared at her. 'It was the best sex of your life,' he declared again, almost defiantly daring her to deny it.

'Okay, I'll give you that.' She cleared her throat. 'But don't you think that's because it was such a fantasy? Like a dream?' Her half-dreaming state had made the memory even better. 'So good it *couldn't* have been real.'

His obsidian gaze narrowed in on her, compelling more explanation from her.

'I didn't know you. You didn't know me.' She faltered. 'We can't ever recreate that scenario.'

'So you think our being together again would be a disappointment?' he asked, incredulous.

'It would have to be,' she muttered. 'Don't you think?'

'No, I don't. You're not curious to know for sure?'

'I…' Of course she was curious. It was hard containing that curiosity. But she didn't want to taint that memory with disappointment, nor did she want to mess up her opportunity at work.

'You liked fantasy sex.'

'So did you,' she defended.

'Yeah,' he admitted with a wolfish grin. 'There are other kinds of fantasy sex.'

She swallowed. 'I'm not into kink.'

He chuckled. 'I can come up with many, many simple, sweet fantasies if you like.'

She licked her lips before realising what a revealing piece of body language she'd instinctively performed. She put her hand to her mouth and rubbed—as if she could deny the yearning there.

'Ellie.'

Oh, help, that had her toes curling, but the rest of her was paralysed. She couldn't walk, couldn't run. She just waited as he took the two paces through the water. So close she had to tilt her chin to maintain eye contact—which she was damn well determined to do. So close she could feel his breath, could feel her own muscles weakening as excitement erupted.

He inclined his head, lowering it almost enough. 'You want fantasy?' His lips barely moved as he challenged.

Ellie couldn't breathe at all now, couldn't hear a thing other than the echo of his words and the amplified thud of her heart. Blood shot to her extremities, her skin suddenly super sensitive. Every *cell* sensitive. And screaming out. Screaming so loud her reason was muted. So she was the one to tilt her chin that tiny bit further, bringing their lips into contact.

She was lost in that instant. She shut her eyes, only able to focus on the velvet warmth of his kiss. The insistence of his lips, his tongue. Oh, she opened, she let him in. She let him, let him, let him. Because what he demanded was exactly what she wanted—passion and need. So swiftly his touch swept her into that burning vortex where thought and caution were flung away because this ecstasy was all that mattered.

With every lush caress of his mouth, her resistance melted. *She* melted, her muscles sliding towards his strength, her mouth moving to welcome his demand. But there was a kernel of tension, slowly knotting, growing, sending the message that only his lips touching hers was not enough. Not nearly enough. She craved closer contact, craved for them to meld completely. Chest to breast, thigh to thigh, for their arms to curl and cling and for them to literally be locked in intimacy. Oh, she wanted that, she wanted that *now*.

She moaned—a song of need, a plea. The pressure of his mouth increased, his tongue flicking in an erotic tease that saw her tremble with it. For her body to move of its own accord—closer, closer, closer. They were inches apart in warm water, she wanted to feel his strong muscles, to press their wet skin together...

'That fantasy enough for you?' he asked, his voice rough as he stepped back. The water splashed as he sat down again on the opposite side of the tub.

Ellie couldn't believe he'd kissed her like that and then let her go. She couldn't believe the intensity in his expression—in his action—had suddenly vanished. 'You're the most awful tease.'

'Actually I think you're the one who can claim that crown,' he argued in that charming rogue way.

'I'm not teasing at all. You're the one who keeps crossing the boundaries.' She swept her sodden hair from her face.

'You keep tempting me to.' He shrugged.

'So it's all my fault?'

'Absolutely.'

Unable to help it, despite knowing it was what he wanted, she laughed.

'You think it's funny?'

She nodded. 'You're so good for a girl's ego.'

'Well, that is my raison d'être.' He inclined his head.

Ellie nodded. Yes, he'd gone back to form—a charming, carefree man made for good humour and good times. Yet she sensed that impenetrable wall only a millimetre beneath his surface.

Damn it, the whole complicated package fascinated her.

CHAPTER SEVEN

'Put these on while we get your things cleaned and dried.'

'I didn't think I'd need more than one pair of jeans. I wasn't expecting a mudbath,' Ellie said with defiance born of embarrassment as she took the jeans and tee Ruben held out to her and then dived to her bedroom to get decent.

She figured that at least he was never going to get off on the 'she's wearing my clothes' thing—they totally swamped her. But suddenly she was feeling decidedly 'his' now wearing his jeans and tee. It was pathetically primeval but utterly seductive.

When she went out to the kitchen he was waiting with two giant mugs of coffee—perfect, as she'd been having some dangerous thoughts about heading to a nearby bed.

'What do you do when you're here alone and the weather's closed in like this?' she asked, desperate to make innocuous conversation.

'I read.'

'Let me guess, thrillers? Gory crime stories?'

'No.' He lifted his mug and led her down the hall-way, pushing open the door to the large, plush study.

He walked to a bookshelf around a corner, further away from the others. 'Non-fiction.'

'Oh, wow.' Ellie gazed at the partially hidden display. Architecture books. Big, expensive, beautiful architecture and design books. Covering all kinds of buildings—not just hotels but homes and castles, inner-city apartments, outback homesteads and skyscrapers. The works.

'You've got a ton.' She moved in front of the shelf and pulled a couple out, then folded to sit cross-legged and opened the first book. It was the perfect safe time-killer.

He followed suit, leaning opposite her, soon burrowed in cushions and flicking through books. They talked, compared favourites, argued about the ugly. Almost two hours passed and Ellie couldn't help thinking that, despite his outrageous flirt moments, his life appeared to be all work.

'So where do you hang out most?' she asked, chuckling when she saw his startled expression. 'Don't worry, I'm not about to start stalking you.'

'At the hotels.'

'But where do you exercise? You play rugby or something?' Surely he was in a team. He totally had the fitness for it.

'I use the gyms in the hotels.'

Oh, of course he did. 'You don't actually have a *home* of your own?'

'There's no point.' He kept flicking pages and didn't look up to answer her. 'I visit the hotels on a constant rotation. I use a room in them. That way I can keep an eye on the quality of the service.'

Ellie glanced around the pristine interior of the place.

'Don't you have any personal stuff?' Aside from archi-tecture books?

'Like what?' he asked absently, still looking at the book spread on his lap.

'Family photos?' *Anything?*

'I have some on my phone.' He shrugged. 'I guess I'm minimalist. I have an office at the chateau but most of the stuff I need is on my laptop.'

'And what do you do for fun?'

'Work is fun.' He looked up and smiled. 'I love what I do. Don't you love what you do?'

'Sure I do. I really do, actually.'

Ruben, now back in position leaning against cush-ions, had a sly look in his eye. 'You're meaning social fun, aren't you?' he asked.

She shrugged as if she weren't *that* interested. 'I'm guessing you enjoy your guests' company.'

'Some more than others,' he answered glibly. 'But not in the way you're thinking. You were an exception and you know it.'

Yes, but nothing could come of the flame between them—there was no future in terms of a *relationship*. She might bring tours here but she could avoid him completely if she wanted to.

Thing was, she *didn't* want to.

But she knew that if she agreed to a fling, when it was over there'd be no contact at all between them. It was how she worked and she was pretty sure it was how he'd work too.

The thought of not ever seeing him again squeezed her vulnerable heart hard. She wanted to see him. She wanted to know how his current deal worked out. She liked hanging out, she liked the aura of freedom he had, she liked how he made her laugh. Yeah, she wanted more of his company and she shouldn't. But if she worked out some boundaries—where she wouldn't give too much and thus not expect too much either—then maybe she could live with it.

'I think we should try to be friends,' she blurted decisively. 'We should put this on a friend level.'

Ruben choked on nothing but fresh air.

'I'm serious.' She smiled as she watched him gasp. 'We have a lot in common. We laugh together. We're similar in that work is important to us. We get on well.'

'And your point?'

She figured she could have him in her life as a friend, or not have him in her life at all. And though she knew she probably *should*, given how attractive she found him, she wasn't ready to cast him out of her life completely. She was still too curious. 'We can be civilised, can't we?'

'There's nothing civilised about the things I want to do with you.'

She closed her eyes for a second and waited for the blood to recede from her cheeks. 'But if we have a fling what do you think will happen in the end?'

He didn't answer.

'What usually happens?' she prompted.

He began to smile, that wry, rueful smile.

'Are you in contact with any of them?' she asked softly.

His shoulders lifted. 'If our paths cross we smile and wave and it's all lovely and amicable.'

'Because they have too much pride to show you how hurt they are inside,' Ellie said dryly.

His brows lifted. 'Honey, I'm not with any one woman long enough for her to get hurt.'

Ellie's laugh came out as a snort but his words made

her all the more resolved—she didn't want too few hot nights, she'd rather have long-term laughs.

'Well, okay, what about you?' he said firmly. 'Are you in contact with your exes?'

As if. 'I haven't had as many as you,' she said pointedly. 'But usually what happens is I have a relationship and, not too long later, the guy moves on. I *used* to try everything to please him, so he'd stick around longer, but I'm not going to bend myself into any more boxes in order to try to keep anyone.' She was never doing that again. 'I don't see any of them any more.'

'So you're not going to bend into any boxes for me?'

She shook her head with a laugh.

'I'm feeling a little insulted,' he said mildly.

'Don't be. Actually you should feel pleased. I want to stay in touch with you.' She really did.

'And that's a first? None of your other men?'

'How many do you think there've been?' She rolled her eyes when she saw the amused look on his face. 'No, I'm not in touch with any of the two hundred and eighty-four. They were jerks.'

He laughed. 'I don't want to be a jerk to you. I like you. I like talking to you.'

'Exactly!' Great, this was easier than she'd thought it would be.

'I still want to have sex with you, though.'

Okay, maybe not so easy. 'You'll get over that.'

'You're saying you're over it?' He moved towards her.

She darted sideways out of reach. 'Look—' she held him off firmly '—everybody says you have to feed passion, indulge it, have so much until you don't want it any more. But the only way to kill a fire is to starve it.'

'And you want to kill it?' He paused, clearly in disbelief.

'Well, that's best, right? Because I don't want us to lose all contact. I like hanging out with you.'

'I don't know whether to be pleased or insulted. You want me to be your buddy?' His unbelieving smile became positively evil. 'How about buddy with benefits?'

'No benefits. Too messy. It would never work.' She was adamant on that.

He stared at her. 'You really want to be friends more than you want to have sex again?' he asked, utterly incredulous.

She inhaled deeply. 'Yes.'

'I don't believe you. In fact I reckon I could get you to change your mind in about a minute or less.'

'If you put your mouth to that task, then I'd probably have to agree with you,' she admitted. 'But then I'd walk out of your life and that would be that. I don't want to have a fling with you. But I do want to be a friend.'

'You're giving me an ultimatum?' He sat an inch from her, clearly astounded.

'Think of it as a challenge.'

'Why would I put myself through that kind of a challenge?'

'How many friends do you have?' she asked, deadly serious.

'I have hundreds of friends.'

'I mean real, true, deep friends?' she asked.

'Friends are friends.' He shrugged off her scepticism. 'I like lots of them.'

'Then this should be easy, right?' she teased.

He sighed. 'You really don't want to be friends with benefits, or even just little perks?'

'That way lies mess and complication. This way lies companionship.'

'Companionship.' He all but spat the word.

'I know there's no such thing as commitment from a guy like you, Ruben.'

He turned into a statue before her eyes.

'To be honest, that's not what I want in my life at this stage either,' she reassured him with a smile. 'Things are exciting for me. I've got this great job with awesome opportunities…' She wanted to focus on succeeding with that.

'Do you really think we can get past the physical attraction?' Ruben really wasn't sure that was going to be possible.

'Sure we can. We're adults, not animals.'

'You like it animal,' he taunted softly, pleased that she still blushed for him.

'You'll forget that, eventually.'

He doubted that very much.

'Are you afraid you're going to fail at this, Ruben?'

Oh, she thought he would, didn't she?

'What do you get out of it?' he asked softly. 'Surely you have other friends already, right? So what is it you get from me that you get from no one else? If it isn't going to be stellar sex, what is it?'

Her flush deepened and she looked away.

He moved closer—not to touch her, but to really see her response. 'Answer me, or I say no to this and get you panting for it in less than a minute. Be honest. What do you get from me?'

'Just that, I guess.' She shrugged. 'I can be as rude as I like with you. I can be honest and you laugh at me and with me. I can completely be myself and it doesn't matter.'

That struck some long-buried nerve deep inside him. 'And you can't do that with anyone else?'

'Not quite the same, no.' She inhaled. 'I don't feel like I have to please you. I don't think I have to do anything but be me with you.'

Ruben looked into her blue eyes, trying to read her. He'd decided never to give a damn what anyone thought of him in life. Ellie's approach couldn't be more different. She cared too much about what people thought—she worked stupidly hard to please them. But it was both a weakness and a strength. It was part of what made her so good at her job, but clearly it had caused her some misery in terms of affairs. And she felt as if she could be free in his company?

Ruben narrowed in on the vulnerability in her blue eyes—and recognised blossoming fear. She was afraid he'd refuse her—that she'd asked for something he didn't want.

And what did he want? To have her in his life for a sex-filled night or two, or for longer as someone to hang with? He tried to think but looking into her eyes was a distraction. They were beautiful—wide and deep, like a vast ocean. Oddly he realised that her wanting just to hang out with him, feeling as if she *could*, made him feel good in a way he'd never felt before. A way that he didn't know how to analyse—couldn't—what with that weird ringing in his ears.

'Saved by the bell,' Ellie was muttering grimly.

Oh, there really was ringing—the doorbell. Ruben took her hand and marched her to the door with him. He didn't want her stropping off to her room because he'd taken too long to answer.

'Ruben?' An older woman stood in the entranceway,

impeccably groomed and dressed in summer country casual. 'I'm so glad you're home.'

'Oh, hi.' He drew a quick breath and put his photographic memory to good use. 'Margot, isn't it?' He'd placed her face—one of the society matriarchs in Queenstown. Lovely woman, very proper, probably wanted something for a good cause. He let go of Ellie and stepped forward to shake the older woman's hand.

'Yes.' She smiled.

'Margot, this is my friend Ellie.' He introduced them coolly, avoiding Ellie's eye as he labelled her the way *she* wanted. 'How can we help?'

'I'd heard you were in residence this weekend and stopped by to remind you of the gala in town tonight. Given you've donated so generously to the hospice, I thought you might like to attend.'

He donated to all the local hospices near his hotels. The care of people in the last stages of cancer in a homelike environment, with family able to be near, was something he felt very strongly about. He and his mother had cared for his father at home, alone. Had a hospice been nearby it might have made some moments almost bearable.

'My donations are supposed to remain anonymous.' He wanted no credit for it. No public recognition. Hell, his business was not built on personality but by private perfection. Quietly satisfied customers were his reward—return customers. He had no hunger for this kind of public approval; his assistance with hospices was intensely personal.

'Yes, and they will remain so.' Margot spoke with soft care. 'I only know about it because I'm the treasurer. But I thought you might like to see how your generosity has helped?' Margot smiled. 'There's a beau-

tiful display at the restaurant and we have a wonderful speaker.'

He cleared his throat. 'Actually, Margot, we're really
tired. We got bogged in the mud for a couple of hours
this morning thanks to this.' He gestured to the damp
fog—it had closed in even more while they'd been in
the study.

'So you'll be spending the night here anyway as the
airport is shut,' she noted brightly. 'Why not come just
for the dinner? It doesn't have to be a late night. It starts
at seven. It would be wonderful to see you there.'

He hesitated and glanced at Ellie. She was watching
him closely. For a second he thought he saw sympathy in
her eyes but she blinked and it was gone. She knew he
didn't feel like socialising tonight. And she was right—
he'd wanted to be utterly alone with her. He'd planned
for them to be miles from anyone up in his mountain
hut away from everything but temptation. The damn
weather had thwarted those plans. And Ellie herself had
thrown Plan B into complete disarray.

Nowadays he often had that nagging question as to
whether a woman was interested in him mainly because of his business interests and accompanying bank
balance. Ellie had been the one perfect exception to
that. She'd had no idea who he was, she'd wanted his
body, then she'd laughed with him. Apparently now she
wanted to be some kind of buddy with him. He didn't
get that at all—figured she'd partly done it because she
didn't think he could. She thought she'd set him an impossible challenge and he understood there was a part
of Ellie that liked to set a challenge. Just as there was a
part of him that loved nothing more than a challenge.
But she had no idea how determined he could be. He'd
taken over a property aged seventeen, for heaven's sake.

He was totally capable of reining in his desires as an adult now. Of course he was…

But he was still looking at her and now a dozen other images flashed in his head.

Okay, the charity dinner wasn't his number one idea of fun but he could see himself failing on the friends thing if he stayed home alone with her tonight. She tempted too much. It would be safer to get out—and prove a point to her at the same time. After all, failure was never an option. And ultimately he had no intention of failing on getting what he really wanted from her. But he'd play it her way for now.

'Of course,' he said, turning to Margot, going for all-out charm. 'Ellie and I would love to be there. Thanks for stopping by.'

Somewhat stunned, Ellie watched Ruben's smile flash to mega-impact. Poor Margot actually reddened, her expression morphing from that of polite hostess to one suffused with genuine pleasure and surprise.

'Oh,' the older woman gasped. 'That's wonderful.' She flicked a glance to Ellie. 'It'll be lovely to have you both there. I'm looking forward to getting to know you better too, Ellie.'

Ellie merely smiled and saved her tongue for when the smartly dressed socialite had slipped back into her silver car and driven away.

'She seems very nice.' Ellie walked into the giant homestead. 'You'll have a great time.'

'You're coming with me,' he called after her, shutting the door behind them.

'No, I'm not.' She smiled sweetly as she shook her head and headed straight for the kitchen for some icy water. 'This is an opportunity for you to spend some time with your neighbours.'

'You're worried because you don't have anything to wear?' he asked. 'There are a bunch of expensive boutiques in Queenstown. We have time to hit them.'

He thought that was why she didn't want to go? 'Oh, please, don't make the mistake of thinking you're going to make me over.' She turned to face him tartly. 'Of course I have something to wear.'

'You only have an overnight bag with you.' He rested his hip against the kitchen counter, watching her fill her glass. 'And you said yourself you don't have a second pair of jeans, that's why you're wearing mine.'

His lascivious look told her he *was* all macho about her wearing his gear. She tried to ignore the hot clench of feminine satisfaction.

'I have a slip that doubles as an evening dress.' She faux demurely took a sip.

His jaw dropped. 'That blue thing?'

Ellie choked as she tried to swallow water while snorting with laughter. How could he sound both scandalised and horn-dog desperate? She shook her head and swallowed safely that time. 'No. Not a slip, it's a dress that doesn't need ironing so I can roll it up. I always have it in the bottom of my overnight bag.'

'What about shoes?'

'I have teeny, tiny strappy numbers. And I have make-up and glittery jewellery too. You never know when you might get that last-minute invite to a red-carpet event.' She was spouting complete rubbish of course—she'd never been to a red carpet event. But she had learnt a trick or two from hanging around on the set of a few ultra-budget short flicks. The make-up artists could work wonders with a tube of Vaseline and an eye pencil. And after the nightmare that had been Nathan and his insulting comments about her at-

tire, she'd gone shopping for a kill-'em-at-any-occasion
dress. And okay, it hadn't been Nathan she'd been thinking of. She'd been channelling her new-found inner seductress—basking in the conquest that had been Ruben
and revelling in supreme sexual confidence for five seconds of madness in the shop's changing room.

'Impressive.' Ruben's expression went evil. 'So you
have no reason to be able to refuse me, then.'

Too late she realised she'd been trapped. Oh, he was
good. There was nothing for it but straight refusal. 'I'm
not going as your date.'

'You have to. We've already told the immaculate
Margot we'll be there and we can't disappoint her now.'

'Look.' She sighed. 'She's thrilled about *you* going.
She won't mind my not being there. You don't need to
do the host thing, I'm happy to have a nice quiet night
here on my own. I'm really tired—it's been an exhausting day out facing the elements, you know.'

'And yet you're going to send me into the wolves'
den, knowing I'm every bit as exhausted.'

'Hardly a den,' she mocked softly. 'They'll welcome
you with open arms.'

'It's a dangerous place, the charity dinner. I'm not
sure you understand the threat I'm facing.' Somehow
he'd moved nearer.

'From all the women throwing themselves at you?'

He nodded soberly. 'It's frightening. I need you to
protect me.'

'Oh, as if.' Arrogant sod. 'You need no protection.
It's the other way round and you know it. You'll be wag-
gling your eyebrows at all the waitresses and they'll
fawn all over you.'

'I only waggle if they've got good racks. Of food.'
He caught her eye and laughed. 'None of those women

need fear me. Come with me. Please. It's what friends do.' He looked sly. 'And you're my *friend* now, right?'

Her eyes narrowed. 'I'd like to think that's possible. It remains to see whether you can manage it.'

'Well, friends support each other, don't they? Here's some truth for you. I'm shy.' He dropped his voice to a whisper. 'I admit it. I like my privacy and I find small talk…difficult sometimes.'

'*Shy?*' she scoffed. 'You're the guy who was happy to stand buck naked in a hotel corridor the morning we met. You're anything but shy. You're outrageous.'

'That was a special occasion.' He stared, all big brown puppy eyes.

'Oh, it was not. You don't care about what people think of you.'

'That's true.' He shrugged off the bashful routine.

Ellie nodded. 'You're stunning at schmooze. You just reduced society matriarch Margot to a blushing, tongue-tied wreck.'

'Doesn't mean I enjoy it. I have good managers at each of the lodges. I don't mix with the clients all that much. I'd rather wander round—'

'Looking like the gardener.'

'Exactly.' He'd edged closer still. 'Go on, come with me.'

She nibbled the inside of her lip, steadfastly ignoring the less than subtle undertone to his invitation. There was that irresistible desire to see what he was like at one of those events—to be out in public with him at her side. To indulge in that dangerous fantasy for a few hours would be far safer than to stay here another night alone with him.

'Okay.' She shrugged, feigning nonchalance. 'I'll go with you.'

'We have a couple of hours before—'

'Yeah, I'm going for a lie down.' She walked, quickly. *'Alone.'*

Two hours later she was running late, having spent too long messing around with all the luxury bathing products in the bathroom and thinking up movie-tour spiels. Wrapped in one of the luxurious robes supplied in the wardrobe, she raced to the kitchen to hunt out a snack. Munching a cracker, she caught him in the corridor on her way back to her bedroom.

She stopped, spilling crumbs as she unconsciously clenched her fist and crushed the cracker. How could any woman think 'friends only' when he looked as sex-in-a-suit as that?

He grinned as if he could read her thoughts. 'You like it?'

Oh, yeah, her *like* was all over her face. Way too late she pulled her jaw from the floor and got her tongue back behind her teeth. 'You're not playing fair.'

'I just thought it might be good to lift the challenge for you. Make you think about what you're giving up.'

As if she needed to think about that any more than she was already.

'You were wrong once—isn't there the possibility you might be wrong twice?' he asked slyly.

'What was I wrong about?'

'That it was fantasy sex that couldn't be repeated. But that kiss in the spa was way better than any fantasy. Just imagine what a whole night together would be like.'

'This is you meeting the friendship challenge, is it?' she asked.

He shrugged negligently. 'Oh, I can meet that challenge. But if you wanted to change your mind at any time, all you have to do is ask.'

And he'd do her? She merely smiled and went to set a challenge of her own. Twenty minutes later she walked into the lounge and waited for his response.

He stared—up and down, up and down, paused just north of her centre, and then up and down again. 'That was really in that tiny overnight bag?'

She twirled. 'It's a tiny dress.'

It was and all Ruben wanted to do was peel it off her. It was black and sleek—like cobwebbing over her breasts and an equally clinging skirt. Her legs were lightly tanned and framed with a pair of barely there sandals on her feet—only a strip of black sequins across her toes and a heel that gave her a slight chance of levelly meeting his gaze.

He managed to haul a couple of words together. 'We'd better go.'

There would have been a couple of hundred people there. The place glittered—diamonds adorned ears, necks, wrists and fingers everywhere. He glanced at Ellie's beautiful skin; diamonds would look good on her. Or sapphires to match her eyes. Although no gem, no matter how precious, could sparkle the way her eyes were now.

She was laughing at how he'd just waylaid a waitress and hoovered too many of her canapés before she'd been able to offer them to anyone else. But honestly, he'd not eaten for ages. The two hours Ellie had had her lie-down, he'd been working.

'You really don't give a damn about what these people think of you, do you?' Ellie teased.

'Why should I? It doesn't matter to me what anyone thinks.'

'But what about your business?'

'It speaks for itself. Each hotel or lodge is its own ad-vertisement. I create them and then disappear into the background. It's not about me. Never about me. People don't go to a luxury retreat to hang out with the owner. They go for space, rest, privacy.' He shrugged.

He watched her talk with one woman about the scen-ery. Snowboarding. Turned out Ellie had never been snowboarding herself, but she got that other woman talking about it for the best part of twenty minutes. She really was interested in what the other was say-ing. Asked intelligent, thoughtful questions. She was so good at listening and paying attention to other peo-ple. At seeming to care. Watching her in action, he re-alised it was the skill set she'd learned as a lonely kid. By giving others attention, she got attention. It made her included.

He watched her show all through dinner. For the most part he just enjoyed her enthusiasm—as did those at their table. But she was interested in being friends with him because she *didn't* have to maintain that viva-cious front the entire time with him. She could be rib-ald. She could be outrageous. She could be tired and grumpy. She could be selfish and take what she wanted. Hell, he wanted her to take what she wanted from him again. His body ached for her to.

Fortunately the band started up. While dancing was a very, *very* risky idea, it was also irresistible.

'Friends kiss each other, don't they?' he asked idly as they barely moved, swaying in the small, heated dance space.

'Oh, you're bad.' Glittering blue eyes sliced through him.

'We're also in a public place, so it's not like we can go overboard. Just a little, friendly kiss.'

'How friendly?'

'Well, given our history, I'd say we're *very* close friends.'

He stole a kiss and felt the fire both sharpen his need and melt his soul. This was what he wanted. Her giving in to him. Wanting him. Hot and sweet and soft. He pulled her closer, ached to have her lush body blanket his. Her warm lips welcomed. Oh, it was good. Blood fired—revitalised—around his body. He actually relaxed, the pressure in his head easing.

But she broke free. 'That was almost overboard,' she muttered, not looking at him.

He nodded but refused to let her out of his hold. Thank heavens for a crowded dance floor.

Ellie was almost out on her feet. No way could she handle more of this dancing and certainly not another 'friendly' kiss. She insisted on heading back to the bar where she stood alongside him and watched him attract people like the Pied Piper summoned every child in his town. He talked with men about farming, sport, politics, building developments. With the women it was more about the hotel business, the restaurants, the local events. Utterly sociable, he was the kind of person hosts loved at a party because he could carry conversation so well.

But it was all safe conversation. She noticed he never talked about himself—all topics were out in the public domain. While she made conversation by talking about the other person, he made conversation by talking about things or events or policies. He never broached the personal with any of them, but was utterly charming. And as the evening wore on it dawned on her that they were at a charity dinner for a hospice and he'd never once mentioned it in any of his conversations here. So that was too personal—she'd suspected so.

But his roguish smile and occasional outrageous joke had so many women giving him that look. And giving Ellie that look of envy.

She fell asleep on the drive home. Ruben pulled into the entranceway and quietly went round the car and opened her door. He scooped her up and carried her inside to the big sofa in the lounge. He didn't want the night to end just yet—not with them going to separate bedrooms.

So much for phases two and three being so easy. No matter the weather problems, the fact was she'd turned the tables on him and somehow he'd agreed to it. *Friends?* It was crazy.

With a soft murmur she stirred, looked at him, all big, blue drowsy eyes. Her heart right there in them— longing. His own heart did a weird flip-flop thing. It wasn't comfortable in the suddenly gaping cavern of his chest. Usually in this situation, when all the blood in his body had rushed south, he'd be on course for some highly satisfactory action. But today, despite the screaming tension from that most masculine part of himself, his brain wouldn't shut down. Amazingly the clarity of his thoughts was more acute than ever. And all he could think was how lovely she was.

'I'm really sleepy,' she said, scratchy-voiced.

'I'm not going to bed without you.' He didn't want to let her go.

'You're not going to bed with me.'

He smiled. A kiss and he'd have her mind changed. The glittering look she gave him beneath her lashes let him know she knew it too. But it had hit him hard—he didn't want to lose her from his life. Not yet. And knowing what he did—of her need for attention, her habit of running from rejection, of her refusal to ever communicate with an ex…not to mention his own dismal track record in maintaining any length of a relationship…

Yeah, now he knew he had to do what she'd asked. Reluctantly. 'Then I guess I'm not going to bed.'

He sat on the sofa, still holding her in his arms. She was soft and warm. He rested his head on hers.

'I had a nice night,' she murmured, settling closer.

So had he. And he was tired and too human to resist the temptation to kiss her again. Her sleepy, soft response deepened. She was deliciously lax in his arms, as if she'd let him do anything. Her breathy moan pretty much confirmed it. But they were friends and while friends kissed, that was all. And frankly? He'd never found kissing so rewarding. Long and luscious, kiss after kiss after way more than friendly kiss.

'Ruben.' She sighed.

He knew she was almost asleep, but she was also begging.

'You could kiss me all kinds of places.' A butterfly whisper.

Utter temptation. She had him so hard. And that was what she wanted, huh? To have her cake and eat it too. Or, more to the point, have him eat it. He smiled at his sleepy wanton woman and couldn't help trailing a finger up her thigh.

Just once. Just once he wanted to *see* her shudder in ecstasy thanks to him. Yeah, he was that selfish. He'd dreamed of it for too long and, breathing in her fresh scent now, there was no resisting. He was touching only a little. Delving into the soft heat. She clenched on him. He rubbed a couple more times and she was there— right there in his arms—vulnerable, beautiful, and, in that moment, completely his. He watched for a moment, but some emotion deep inside drove him to kiss her, to catch the last of her sighs, to inhale her energy.

The ache tearing him apart inside wasn't purely sexual. The craving ran too deep to be only that—but it was a yearning for something he couldn't ever admit wanting. So he clamped it—shutting it down, forcing his own need away.

Breathing hard, he looked at her peaceful expression. She was both vulnerable and strong. His sharp clarity returned. He didn't want her trying to bend into a box to keep any fling with him going. He had no illusions that a fling wouldn't end. Of course it would. In the past, a woman in a relationship with him soon grew tired—of his long absences due to constant travel, his mental and emotional absences. Ellie would soon get to the point where she'd had enough. She'd get mad and shout how selfish he was. How he didn't care.

Frankly he didn't want to care.

But he didn't want Ellie walking out on him in anger. She recognised his faults already. Knew what would happen. So she was removing that eventuality with immediate effect because she didn't want to lose touch with him altogether. She didn't want to disappear in the sunrise as another one-night stand. There was something in him she liked and wanted—other than sex.

And maybe all that was, was his acceptance of everything she was, without question or criticism. And he felt a simple honesty in return—he didn't want to screw her over. He didn't want to let her down. That was the last thing she deserved. And the only way he could ensure he wouldn't was to do as she'd asked.

CHAPTER EIGHT

ELLIE woke in a crumpled but cosy ball. Stretching out of it was the problem, given her muscles were stiffer than they'd been the day before. Half beneath her was Ruben, toppled sideways on the sofa, still in his tux and destined to have a hellish crick in his neck

They'd spent their first *almost* platonic night together. There'd been that sleepy kissing session and that moment just before she fell so deeply into sleep—the teasing luxury, the supposed relief he'd given her.

But it was no relief at all. It was like having the merest taste of some decadent gateaux that was now locked behind a glass cabinet and for ever out of bounds. All she could do was look at it with longing. Yeah, she wanted to devour the gateaux now—to indulge in every last bit. She could feel his hard length pressed against her thigh. Who was she kidding about the 'friends' thing? The desire to have him was too intense. 'Ruben?'

His eyes opened, his gaze warm and drowsy. Only as he woke he blinked a couple of times and a cool veil slipped down, masking that expression. She didn't like it.

She shifted her thigh so his thick erection pressed closer into her softness. 'You failed already.'

He shook his head. 'You're the one who got the "ben-efit" last night.'

'You teased me into it.' He was tempting her delib-erately again now—wasn't he?

'You asked me to kiss you in the most inappropriate places,' he said softly. 'I was a complete gentleman.'

'With your hand in my pants?'

'You wanted my mouth there,' he countered. 'I went with the less intimate option.'

Oh, it was *all* intimate. Excitement skittered through her. Yes, the friends idea was a failure already...

'We'd better get going,' he said crisply, dropping his gaze from hers. He shifted slightly so he was no longer so intimately against her.

She slid off him—withdrawing too, chilling as she realised he wasn't out to tease her. He really was draw-ing the line she'd asked him to. 'You're so right. We had.'

Ruben drove them to the airport. It wasn't as foggy as the day before but it was still grey and wet. No doubt the flight would be bumpy. She sighed as they pulled up outside the terminal. The heartfelt sound gave away more than she meant it to.

'It'll be no problem,' he said, his hands tightly grip-ping the steering wheel.

'Of course,' she said, not believing it at that point in time. 'I'm off on a four-day tour next week.'

'I'm heading up to Taupo in the latter half of the week.'

'So there we go,' she said breezily, covering the ache of his absence that was already twisting her heart. 'Physical distance will take care of any last little itch.'

'Absolutely.'

'Don't come in, you can just drop me,' she said as he pulled into a park.

'Okay,' he answered readily. 'I'll be in touch.'

She wondered if that was a line. If the whole 'sure we can be friends' agreement had just been him being charming and polite to get through the weekend. Now she had some info for work, there was no reason for him to contact her directly again. He could do all the negotiations with Bridie and be absent if ever Ellie came on tour here. What a fool she'd been. She should have just taken his body for the weekend and been done with it, because she'd probably never hear from him again once she'd stepped from his car.

He seemed to read her doubts. 'I *want* to be friends.' He leaned across the car to brush a lock of her hair from her face. 'Truth is I like you. I had fun.'

'So did I.'

And not *that* kind of fun. Of course now the trouble was the yearning, for that was all she could feel right now. Especially after that sweet kissing session last night—those deep kisses had turned her heart completely inside out. It was one thing to have dynamite, animal sex. It was another to have tenderness and quietness and restraint. That had showed respect.

At the time she hadn't wanted it, but it had been *respect*, not rejection, that had stopped him from going down on her. From taking everything she'd been offering in her most vulnerable moment. She got out of the car quickly and didn't look back. She was in enough trouble without a longing parting glance.

Fortunately in the modern age there was that safe way to communicate—the text message. Where you could send just the smallest of sentences and wait to see what—if any—response you got. She was completely overthinking it already, mentally composing some silly thing she'd write the first time. Wondering again whether he'd even reply or whether he'd just been going along with her 'friends' idea merely for form's sake over the weekend...

Just as she was rolling her eyes at her own pathetic thoughts her phone chimed. She read the text right away.

Is it within friend boundaries to say I miss you already? Can't stop thinking about you.

She smiled and tapped out her reply.

No, I think that's ok. Friends do miss each other.

Yeah but you don't know what it is I'm thinking about doing with you.

That's possibly too close to the boundary.

I like to bend boundaries.

Ellie flexed her feet to rid even a fraction of the amount of tension from her overwrought body. He was hopeless. But even so, she was happier to have him as a hopeless charmer than not at all.

I'm turning my phone off, my flight's about to depart.

Ellie managed not to turn her phone back on after she'd landed—not 'til she was home and in her pyjamas and had one of her fave films loaded. It rang a mere five minutes later.

'Are you watching a movie?' He obviously heard it playing in the background.

She chuckled. 'Yes.'

'What is it?'

'Casablanca.'

'What happens?'

'You've never seen it?'

'No. Tell me about it.'

Somehow they ended up talking for over an hour.

* * *

A week and a half later Ruben lay back in bed and touched her name on his phone. He'd called her almost every night. He hadn't meant to, but it was so easy. Just a quick call for an update. It was always just before sleep time, in that most quiet of moments when he was alone in his room and she was all he could think of. She'd gone on tour again and had him in hysterics nightly with her descriptions of her clients and the way they were getting on with each other. He was looking forward to the latest anecdotes.

But part-way through the week, reluctant to break the connection too soon one night, he'd ended up talking to her about his own work. The deal was almost sealed—two more properties added to his collection and a million more hassles to work through. He confessed them to her—he, who'd worn all the worries alone for years, now found himself telling her the most stupid small details. She listened, she laughed and somehow helped him cut through the burden. She was a good listener. But it didn't make him want to see her any less.

'I'm flying back into Wellington on Monday. You want to do lunch next week?' he asked as soon as she answered his call. He wanted lunch on Monday but he was trying to keep it casual. Not desperate. They were friends now, so the driving need to see her could just ease off—yes?

'Oh, I can't, sorry, not going to be here.'

He sat bolt upright. 'Where are you going?'

'I'll be on the road again, back-to-back tours.'

'Damn it, Ellie, you've got to be kidding me.' Pissed off, he flung back the covers and got out of bed to pace. 'Why back to back? You'll be exhausted.'

'I'll be fine. It's fun. I'll call you.'

Yeah, but that wasn't quite enough. He found himself

thinking of her all the time. Wanting to tell her things, filing them away for when he called her. Wishing she could see his new place. Wanting to hear her ideas on what could be done with it.

'So how's your inspection going?' She filled the silence that had grown too long.

'Okay. A few staffing issues but then there always are. We can work through them. It's a stunning location. It's very different from the chateau and the lodge but just as beautiful. I think you'll love it.'

Now she took her time answering. 'I'm sure everyone will. You have a talent for spotting places that people will be drawn to.'

He wanted her to be drawn there—like the way she'd been drawn to both the chateau and the lodge. 'You must be tired from the last tour.' He knew just how much of herself she poured into those. There was no perfunctory checking names off a clipboard, she basically put on a show for the people. 'You should have a break.'

'I'm okay. It's nice to be busy,' she answered breezily. 'I'm really enjoying the work. Want to take up any opportunity Bridie gives me.'

'Don't let her take advantage of you.'

A low laugh. 'I won't.'

Eight days later Ellie's phone buzzed with yet another text message. He'd developed a skill for random comments during the day. Ellie was now in the habit of having her hand in her pocket, holding her phone, ready to answer instantly. But just as she was answering the text, he actually called. Unfortunately it was just as she was waiting for some stragglers to get to her bus.

'Aren't you flying to Auckland this afternoon?' She didn't bother saying hello.

'Yes, but I wanted to tell you about—'

'Nope, go pack or something,' she said.

'You're cutting me off?'

'Yes, I have a tour group waiting for me.'

'Oh, okay, I'll call you later.'

She put her phone back in her pocket and smiled at her waiting people—ignoring the fluttering buoyancy of her heart. But it was lifted high on that confidence that when she called back he'd be there to listen. And talk right back to her. She loved the way he talked to her about his work now, how familiar they were with what was going on in their lives. She was getting the hang of handling his friendship—sure she was.

'Ellie.'

She was properly awake in an instant. 'Is something wrong? It's the middle of the night.'

'I was thinking about you.'

She smiled but said nothing. She'd been thinking about him too. She clutched the phone closer and burrowed more into her warm bed.

'Ellie?'

'I'm here.' She giggled at the hint of belligerence in his tone. 'Have you been drinking?'

'No.' Defensive to the extreme. A sigh. 'I just can't get to sleep and I'm so tired.'

'Make yourself a mug of warm milk,' she said wryly.

'It's too hot here for milk.' He groaned, not appreciating her tone. 'It's really hot.'

'Turn on the air conditioner.'

'It's too noisy.'

'So you thought you'd ring me instead, at 3:00 a.m. Little bit spoilt of you, Ruben.'

'What can I say? I was an only child.'

She heard the smile then. Smiled back in response but was glad he wasn't there to see just how easily he brought her onside.

'You ever had phone sex?' he asked.

Boom. Lightning hit her heart, instantly sucking her into an intimate vortex. 'Are you sure you haven't been drinking?'

'Just answer the question.'

'No, I think I'd get the giggles.' Honesty prevailed.

'Yeah.' He chuckled. 'We could always have Skype sex. Then we'd get the visuals. I know you like a movie.' Oh, he was wicked.

And it had been weeks since her last orgasm. 'Except I don't have one of those fancy smart phones with the camera and all.'

'I could buy you a smart phone.'

She didn't want him to buy her anything. 'Ruben.'

'Yes?'

'We're supposed to be friends and not having any kind of sex.' She knew down to the hour how long it had been and, no, it wasn't getting easier. But it would. Sure it would.

'Oh, hell,' he muttered. 'I forgot about that.'

'Obviously.'

'I'll try harder.' He sounded contrite.

'Yeah, you need to try much, *much* harder.'

'Yeah,' he answered softly. 'You like it hard.'

'Ruben,' she warned him. Biting her lip because, hell, yes, she'd liked it hard from him.

'What'll you do to me if I slip up again?'

Slip up? Oh, yeah, she could think of the exact thing he'd slip up and into her.

'I'm sure I could come up with a suitable punishment.' Oh, this was ridiculous. She was getting turned on by the slightest smut talk? 'I'll find some way of restraining you.'

So many ideas of restraint just flooded her head. She heard the faintest strangled sound and smiled. She wasn't the only one sensing the innuendo.

'What if I fight back?' he asked softly. Ominously. 'You know I do like to tease. And I can keep that up for a long, long time.'

'You'd want to draw it out?' She slid lower into her bed. Her toes scrunching, trying not to let her hips flex the way they were begging to.

He sighed—oh, it was more of a groan. She could hear the sensual ache in it. Her hands yearned to touch, to relieve both of them.

'Draw out and then push back in. Deep. Over and over,' he muttered so soft. No double talk now. Direct, so close to dirty. And devastating. 'I keep seeing you...' His sentence drifted.

She bit her lip, her need to know overwhelming. Her hidden aches opening wide again. 'Seeing me what?' She hardly formed the words.

'You like my hand between your thighs.'

She sucked in a shocked breath.

'You do,' he insisted. 'It's one of your favourite things. It makes you come.'

She couldn't deny it.

'Do you wish my hand was there now?'

She rolled slightly, closing her eyes as she sank deeper into the bed—deeper into the half-dreamland he was conjuring with those low words.

'I know how hungry you are. How impatient you get,' he said, relentless now in his seduction. 'You have your hand between your thighs now, pretending it's mine.'

She gripped the telephone receiver harder. Her other hand curled exactly where he said, unable to resist the temptation.

'I know what you're going to do,' he said.

'What would that be?' She clenched her upper thighs together hard. The tension spiked her need higher. Every sense sharpened—her hearing acute, her skin a receptor of pleasure.

A soft pause, enough for her to sense this was no tease now. He was sharing an intimate truth—his private fantasy—and entwining it with hers. So intensely personal.

'You think of me. You can't help but touch.'

She'd been holding her breath so long, now a tiny gasp escaped.

'You have to touch. You touch where you want me to touch you. How you want me to touch you.'

She screwed her eyes tighter at the intimacy in his tone. The assurance of that direction. 'And what do you do?'

Another deep sigh. 'I want to watch, to listen, but I want to touch too. And then all I can think of is you riding me hard.' He swore. 'You rode me so good.'

Ellie trembled, holding back the release that was a single stroke away. They were having unintentional, accidental phone sex? How had that happened?

She turned her burning cheek, shifted her damp body onto a cool stretch of cotton sheet. Absorbing the chill, desperate to restore sanity. 'Ruben,' she whispered. 'I have to go now.'

'Ellie,' he whispered back.

'Yes?'
'Dream of me.'
She had been for weeks. Every damn night.

CHAPTER NINE

HE DIDN'T call for a couple of days, which was frankly a record. And the next time he did, she knew there was something they needed to get in the open if this was ever going to work out. She darted to the nearest bathroom for some privacy to talk to him, staring at her pale, sleep-lacking skin in the mirror.

'You know that if…if you meet up with someone else, you don't have to keep it secret from me. You can tell me. Okay?' She held her breath.

His answer was so long coming she'd nearly turned blue.

'Okay,' he said slowly. 'Same for you.'

'Of course.' She breathed out painfully. As if she could meet anyone as gorgeous as him.

'Have you met up with anyone else?' he asked.

'No. No.'

'Nor have I.'

She licked very dry lips. 'I know you have needs, Ruben. I'm not going to be…bothered. We're friends now.' As much as she'd hate it, maybe it would be better if he did hook up elsewhere. Then the agony of waiting for that nightmare would be over.

Again he took his time replying. 'And you'll tell me if you do?'

She laughed. 'I'm off the market for now. This job is taking up all my time. It's what I want to focus on for the next while.'

'What about your needs?'

She hesitated, hadn't meant for this conversation to be about *her* at all. 'I haven't got time to think about them.'

'Maybe you should think about them or they might sneak up on you again.'

She bit her lip, glad he couldn't see how she'd now gone red in the face—how her blood was zinging all round her damn willing body. 'That night in the chateau was a once only.'

'Yeah, and I don't think I'm ever going to forget it.'

It had been over three weeks since he'd last seen her and he'd thought he had it all under control. He'd been wrong on that.

'Hey,' he said as he got to her table—supposedly they were to have lunch. But it was crazy the way his pulse was pounding.

Her smile couldn't have been more rewarding. Her eyes glittering—deeper in colour than he remembered. She sparkled. And he had nothing under control. The less he saw of her, the more he thought of her. It wasn't supposed to be that way at all. Wasn't the maxim 'out of sight, out of mind'? But she was more than in his mind, she was in his body and in what little soul he had.

She was wearing jeans—heaven help him—with a white blouse and as she looked up at him he could see the lace edge of her bra. He'd become that much of a randy schoolboy he was reduced to sneaking glimpses down her shirt. It took only a second to decide to put the full plan into action. He'd suffered enough. And so too had she. He noted the flare in her eyes, the colour in her cheeks deepen, and, yes, he noticed the way her breasts responded to his less than subtle appreciation of them.

So he didn't sit down. Instead he extended his hand to pull her out of her seat. 'I've got a surprise for you.'

'What is it?' A flutter of caution cooled Ellie's pleasure at seeing him again because he didn't look that excited, if anything he looked more serious than she'd ever seen him. The edges of his beautiful mouth were held firm, not forming their natural curve up.

'There was a vital part of the station that you didn't get to see.'

'The station?' He was half dragging her out of the café and into his convertible. 'We're not going to the station.'

'Plane leaves in thirty, we've got just enough time to make it.'

'Ruben, we're only having *lunch*. I can't just go from work—'

'It's all arranged with Bridie. She's taking the tour this afternoon.'

'What?'

'You've worked too many days in a row anyway. You have to have a break some time.'

Ellie gazed at him. She was sure there was more to this, but he wasn't offering any deeper explanation this second.

It was less than an hour's flight from Wellington to Queenstown and he spent most of it typing into his phone. Not to be outdone Ellie read the inflight mag cover to cover. Once on the ground they didn't get into a car; instead he led her across the airfield to a helicopter.

'Ruben, I don't have any spare clothes with me.' She finally broke the silence.

He turned and looked at her—the old, utterly outrageous Ruben with that wicked smile and knowing expression. 'Sweetheart, you're not going to need any.'

With a stumble Ellie all but slithered into the helicopter. What had happened? There was no mistaking his intention now. Where on earth was he taking her?

The tragic thing was, she didn't much care. She was too excited to be back in his company and to know the spark was still as strong for him as it was for her. Hell, if anything it was worse. And this was him fighting for what he wanted.

Neither spoke while he flipped switches and made the rotor blades whirl. They still weren't loud enough to drown the din of her pulse in her ears.

She'd been in a helicopter before but not one as light as this or as plush inside. They zoomed, over the plains, heading further south, the mountains to their right. Then he pointed out the lodge so she got her bearings. He flew super low to follow the river in the valley, then up high, so close to the mountains, a breath away from the splash of a towering waterfall...

But she sat completely still in her seat. Her pulse slammed, her thoughts disordered—anticipation screwing with her head. They flew over one mountain, deeper into the range and there, hidden from possible view from anywhere other than the air, was an alpine lake. One of those that belonged in ancient myth and legend. Steely blue and still. He brought the helicopter down, landing on a small smooth edge.

'Come on,' he invited her.

He'd been here many times before, she could tell, and she totally got why. It was the most amazing colour, reflecting the cold clarity of the sky. It really was the scene from some ancient mystical, alternate world story—just like the movies. Only real. Fantastically real.

'It's beautiful.' It was so awe-inspiring she couldn't think of any words to fully describe the reaction within her. The reality of pure, unadulterated fantasy.

'It's also icy cold so don't dive in, because I don't want to have to jump in and rescue you.'

She laughed, glad he'd lightened the intensity. And yes, she did have the urge to dive in. It looked so inviting and, hey, maybe it would cool her burning senses.

She found a small flat stone and tried skimming it across the lake. He foraged in the short tussock for more and they had a contest for a while. And all that while—longer really—her ability to resist him curled into a smaller and smaller ball.

'We haven't talked about it,' he said, aiming another flat pebble across the lake.

'About what?'

'That phone call.'

She felt the flush ripple like a wave from her toes to the tip of her scalp. 'Oh.'

Oh was right—the guy had turned her on to nuclear with nothing but a few suggestions. Phone sex—a total first.

'It's not going to happen.'

'What?' she asked, confused.

'You being with anyone else.'

Oh, he meant *that* conversation?

'No one else, Ellie.' He turned to face her—all arrogance. 'You know you can't. Not until you've had enough of me.'

Oh, that wasn't fair—what if she'd *never* had enough of him? Because he'd have enough of her all too soon, she just knew it.

'So you have a choice to make.'

'I do?'

'Uh-huh.' He turned and skimmed another stone across the water. It bounced seven times. 'We could stay up here the night.'

'Where?'

'Just beyond that ridge there's a hut.'

This was why he'd brought her to an utterly isolated spot. Because he wanted…what *she* wanted.

'We could spend the night up here or we could go back to the station in the helicopter. I should warn you there's only one bed in the hut and it's not very big.'

Ellie's brain whirled—and then she stared up at the completely blue sky. 'It looks to me like there's a storm coming. It might be safer to stay up here.'

He walked towards her, holding her gaze imprisoned in his despite shaking his head. 'No storm, Ellie. No games. Just be honest. Do you want another night with me or not?'

Oh, his whole approach was outrageous. Excitement scudded in her belly, her innermost muscles stretching and flexing already. 'What kind of a question is that?'

'Just answer it.'

What did he want, her acquiescence written in blood? Or perhaps sweat? 'Okay, take me there.'

The chocolate-brown eyes were scorched. 'You're sure.'

'Yes.' She knew what she was doing. They were hardly lost in a snowstorm and forced to cling close to preserve life. This was a decision. *Her* decision. And she was tired of fighting the need.

He turned abruptly, climbed back into the helicopter. Ellie walked back towards the lake. It wasn't too late to change her mind but her mind and body were in sync already—she knew what she wanted.

Ruben got what he needed from the chopper and walked back to where she waited. It felt good to have her in place, ready to meet him. He drank in the signs— yeah, her blue eyes were deepening, just like the sky above them. She kept that intense eye contact, as if she was trying to see through him. His heart pounded—he briefly wondered if she could hear it, because he didn't like to be looked at that closely.

'Promise me something,' she said with that husky voice that gripped his attention completely. 'This one night. That's all. Nothing more afterwards. When we get back to civilisation, we're back to where we were. Just friends again. That's the only way this can happen. The fantasy, right?'

'Why do you keep trying to control this?'

'I'm not—'

'This isn't going to go away unless we deal with it. Your way isn't working.'

'One night.'

'The *whole* night.' He pressed his end of the bargain home. 'Not just once and then sleep. I want literally the whole, damn night.' Though he feared even that wasn't going to be enough.

'All night?' She paused, her tongue slipping over her lips.

She honestly thought they'd have just the once? Oh, she hadn't a clue. But she was on the edge. He stepped closer to her, acutely aware of the shifting signals— her shortened breathing, her flush, her almost invisible shiver. Oh, yes, it was going to be more than once. He'd get her over that line again and again. But he needed all night to do it. So they could leave tomorrow as ex-lovers, over this intensity, leaving no burning anxiety left. No more of this desire that had twisted him inside out the last few weeks.

Ellie was embarrassingly close to orgasm just from the suggestion of sex. And only a few steps into the walk to the hut she stumbled.

'Something's hurting?'

She shook her head. Nope, it was the unchecked wanton, wicked, desperate thoughts that had caused her loss of co-ordination. 'I'm fine.' She just wanted to be at the damn shack already.

He'd stopped and now stared stonily at her. Once more that uptilt of his mouth had flattened out to a thin line. Suddenly he lunged.

'What are you doing?' she shrieked.

In a blur and a thud he'd gone in low and hard and she was upside down. His grip was firm but apparently effortless given the pace he was striding up the mountain.

'What. Are. You. Doing?' She added some outrage to the question.

'Stopping you from doing yourself an injury.'

'Oh, please, this is just you unable to keep your hands off me.' Oh, yeah, and her excitement had just quadrupled.

'That too,' he confirmed, unapologetically running his hand up the back of her thigh and grabbing a handful of her butt.

'Well, put me down. You'll do *yourself* an injury.' She was no lightweight.

'We're nearly there anyway.'

'Ruben, seriously. I'm getting giddy.'

He squeezed her butt, then shifted, wrapping both arms around her as he slid her down his body to set her on her feet. For a moment she leaned against him, needing that closeness. All her personal space was his and, oh, it was good.

'Turn around.' He laughed.

'How do you expect me to when you're holding me so tight?' She was more breathless than he, which was embarrassing given he'd been the load bearer.

He turned her, holding her firm, pulling her body back close against his as soon as he could.

She drew an even deeper breath. '*That's* the hut?'

'Uh-huh.' As he laughed again she felt his chest rumbling against her back.

She smiled too, gazing at the small building, not hiding her amazement. 'So what are we doing here, glamping?' Glamour-camping. In by helicopter to a pristine lake and then a little trek to some deluxe boudoir?

'Hey, it's hardly five stars—look at the place. It's tiny and made out of tin,' he said in mock-defence. 'But we can get it really warm.'

Oh, she bet they could.

It *was* tiny, no more than a couple of metres squared. Two-storeyed and on stilts. A beautiful copper coloured tower. He strode ahead, pulling a set of keys from his pocket. He unlocked the padlocks on each side and pulled up the shades so they became awnings, revealing the massive windows beneath providing a view as far as the eye could see in each direction.

'Oh, my.' Ellie peered in the first window.

There was a log burner on the ground floor, with a pot on the top, a rug, a cupboard with a small amount of supplies—survival food, coffee. No sofa, just a wooden floor and a mountain of cushions. But that was what made it so damn glamorous. The wooden floor was polished, the rug hand woven, the cushions covered with the most expensive fabrics.

'You bring people here often?' Oh, she suspected him.

He shook his head. 'No. Honestly no.' His smile twisted. 'Let me get the fire going.'

It already was—a roaring inferno in her belly. 'You're not going to rub two sticks together?'

'Well, you only need one when it's a match.'

She kicked off her boots, as he did, and followed him inside.

'I'm guessing trampers and members of the public don't use this.' Every single item in the place was carefully selected, chosen for both use and quality, neat and tidy and perfect.

'No, it's not on any maps. It's my little getaway.'

'It's pretty amazing.' She turned around, taking it all in.

He waved a hand, encompassing that tiny space. 'You really like it?'

'Absolutely.' How could anyone not?

He looked boyishly, endearingly pleased. 'I designed it.' He coughed. 'And built it.'

'Really?'

'Is that so hard to believe?' He actually looked self-conscious.

Of course it wasn't. She suspected he was capable of many things, given all he'd achieved in the last ten or so years. 'You've designed other things?'

'Just this. It was all I wanted just for me.'

He owned several luxury lodges—massive ones—and he'd built himself a tiny annexe up in the wild heights.

'Have you brought any other women here?' She

shouldn't want to know this. Knowing this was irrelevant. But somehow it mattered.

He shook his head and too much satisfaction burned through Ellie's veins.

'Truth is I've never brought anyone here. I like being alone, appreciating the view. It's peaceful.'

Yes, this place offered serene simplicity. 'I'm not breaking that peace for you?'

'You're part of the fantasy.' He smiled. 'I think everybody needs an escape.' He bent to get the fire going.

'Especially those rich people who have it so hard,' she teased.

'Well, them no less than any other people. And they may want privacy and luxury furnishings. This is *my* escape.'

It was two square metres of heaven. An earthbound spot for angels to come down and enjoy the majesty of the Alps.

'But it really isn't glamping,' he muttered apologetically. 'The facilities are…uh…there.' He jerked his head to a spot out of the window where she could see a shovel. Beyond that, the privacy of tussock land.

'Great.' She grinned.

'There's a tap, the tank collects the rain water from the roof. There's some soap and stuff in the cupboard.' He stood. 'Come up and see the view before the light goes altogether.'

The flue of the log burner ran up the wall—radiating heat already—and further along from that was the ladder.

On that second floor there was a bed—not a giant bed, only slightly larger than a single and currently stripped of coverings. The walls were wooden, warm and cosy. There was only one window up here—a large rectangle cut out, facing the best view right up the spine of the Alps. While some might have wanted glass all round, like the lower level, the one window was like a painting. A frame for nature's greatest effort. It gave the eye a focal point, but the rest of the room offered a sense of safety, of security against that awesome, but ultimately uncaring environment. It really was a nest.

'It must be amazing here in the rain.' She'd love to lie in that bed and listen to a storm lash the tin.

'Yeah.' He pulled out an underbed storage box, opening it swiftly.

'There are sheets?' She laughed. She didn't know whether to be insulted that he hadn't jumped on her already, or touched that he was concerned for their comfort.

He looked a little sheepish. 'I get too hot in sleeping bags.'

She watched him flare the sheet out over the mattress.

'Told you it wasn't the world's biggest bed.' He grimaced.

She ran her hands down her thighs to stop the sudden damp nerves. 'Can I help?' She couldn't believe he was being so matter of fact and restrained about this, especially after the cave-man toss-her-over-his-shoulder approach of earlier.

'Pillows.' He nodded to the box in the corner.

She opened it and smiled. 'How many pillows do you need?'

He pulled a handful of pillowslips from the linen box and threw them at her. 'I *like* pillows.'

'So it's not just for the luxury look at the lodge?' She quickly covered a few and tossed them onto the now sheet-covered bed. 'How many do you have on your bed?'

He shrugged. 'Enough.'

'You cuddle a pillow,' she teased.

'At least it's not a soft toy,' he said, defensively snappy.

She giggled.

'I'm going to show you just how useful a couple of extra pillows can be,' he threatened.

Ellie swallowed, her toes curling in her socks.

'Except we should probably eat something first.'

Oh, he just *had* to be kidding. Was he deliberately torturing her? She shook her head and pushed her hands into her jeans pockets. 'I'm not very hungry.'

She wanted action. She wanted to be done with the ache that had haunted her so long. She wanted to burn the memory of that night. So she undid the first button of her blouse, then the second.

For a moment, he watched her. Then—to her relief—he moved. She smiled, hoping he was going to take over; she wasn't entirely comfortable with her attempted striptease. But to her surprise he moved only to switch on the battery-powered lantern that hung in one corner.

She paused. Completely self-conscious now.

'Oh, no,' he murmured. 'Don't stop. I didn't have the pleasure of seeing you last time.'

She couldn't.

He smiled. And that was when she saw the sheen of sweat on him—the film of heat that hadn't been there even after he'd lugged her up the mountain for five minutes. No, this sign of tension in him was new. And empowering. 'Only if you do the same for me.'

His wickedness flashed. 'You want me to strip for you?'

'Oh, yes.' She undid the last buttons and let her shirt fall. 'I go no further until you've matched me.'

She hadn't even blinked before that 'Lucky' tee shirt was whisked over his head and on the floor already. He unfastened his jeans. To her delight, he didn't take his briefs down with the denim. They were the close-fitting knit boxer type. They fitted him well.

'This is all for you, Ellie.' He knew exactly where she was looking.

'You and your size thing,' she mumbled.

'I'm not the one with body-conscious issues,' he taunted softly. 'But trust me,' he said. '*Look* at me. Look at what you do to me. I want you so much it hurts.'

And she wanted it all.

'So now it's your turn,' he said.

She slipped out of her jeans, taking her socks off—but, like him, leaving that last layer.

'Lace.' He nodded. 'Like your slip that night.' His gaze roved over her. 'You like the feel of it?'

'I like the feel of you.' She stepped towards him.

'Uh-uh.' He shook his head and backed a pace. 'It's not going to be quick this time.'

She needed it to be. She wanted that orgasm so badly. She licked her lower lip, so hot, so ready. So wanting. And given the pressure the front of his briefs was under, he was too. And so she went to the bed, removing her bra in the two paces it took to get there. She slipped off her knickers and stretched out on the mattress. Daring him to deny her now.

His grin disappeared for a moment as he watched her recline. Good, it was about time he felt as bothered as she was. Only then, to her surprise, his smile came back—more wicked than ever. He leaned over and took her hand, pulling her to sit up.

'Are you sure you don't want to star in a movie, Ellie?' he asked quietly.

'What?' Why wouldn't he just hurry up and lie down with her?

'Look at the window.' His voice a wicked tease, an invitation to decadence.

The night sky was now black—the moon had waned to the thinnest of crescents that threw little light. The stars not bright enough to fight back against the glow of the lantern in their room. So the window reflected the scene within—it had become a mirror.

'No one can see us. There isn't anyone for miles,' he said between teasing kisses everywhere on her face but her mouth. 'But we can see us. You can see us. You can watch.' He stepped in front of her, turned his back to the window and dropped to his knees.

She put her hand to her mouth when she saw what he meant. The clarity of their images. She was transfixed.

'Life-size screen,' he muttered, pressing a kiss to her throat.

He had to feel how her heart was racing. 'Ruben…'

'The lantern stays *on*,' he said firmly. 'The lantern stays on all night.' It was a decree. 'I want you to know it's me.'

That stabbed. 'I know that already.'

'*All* night,' he reiterated firmly. And then he kissed lower—down her neck, across her collarbones.

And she watched. Excitement liquefied her bones. Her body went as lax as a doll—his to toy with. Oh, yeah, she was starring in her own blue movie.

She licked her dried lips. 'I've never watched this kind of movie before.'

'Time you did.' He reached her breasts. 'But only with me.'

'Ellie Summers, porn star.'

'Ellie Summers, ultimate temptation.' He thumbed her taut nipple and looked up at her sceptical expression. 'You don't believe me?'

'I think you're quite good at saying nice things.'

'I'm quite good at doing nice things too. Things that feel nice.' He returned to task.

'Oh, my,' she breathed.

'You've never watched a woman be pleasured?'

'You're wicked.' Heat flushed through her.

'Watch while I do that for you,' he muttered.

'Oh.'

She'd never been very visual when it came to sex. She liked it in the dark, under the covers, the wobbly bits mostly out of the way. But the temperature in here was scorching—there was no way she wanted a sheet on her. And seeing a guy this built, on his knees in front of her. Yeah, that played to her hitherto unknown inner exhibitionist. She liked it. She liked what he was doing even more.

He cradled her breasts in his hands as if they were treasures he'd spent centuries searching for. His hands stroked down her sides, his palms flat, his reach broad and sure. He held her hips still as he bent forward to kiss her—from breast to breast, down her sternum. She lifted her hands, ran her fingers through his hair—so simple, but it was what she desired most. His kisses made her tummy tauten. His grip on her hips firmed as she unconsciously began to rock nearer him.

His smile was pleased. 'Getting warmer?'

She shook her head. 'Need more.'

She watched him tending to her, drank in the play

of muscles across his broad back. His body was beautiful—big in the right places, but lean so that definition
could be seen. His butt taut, muscles clenching as he
thrust his hips slightly in time to his nips and kisses on
her breasts. Oh he was gorgeous. He reached to cup her
other breast as his tongue lashed her nipple. She felt like
a prized lover, in the care of masculine perfection. She
lifted her gaze and looked at her own face. The flush
in her cheeks, the heavy-lidded darkness of her eyes.
The full-lipped smile, her skin grazed by his stubbled
jaw. She looked the picture of hedonism. And he was
her expert, demanding slave.

'You know I'll do anything you want.' He paused
to look up at her.

Oh, yeah, captive lover. Her lungs were drawing in
pure fire. 'Everything.' And now, because she was almost there already.

She put her hands on the top of her thighs, rubbing
hard—applying pressure herself to try to ease the ache
there. The desperate need for the pleasure of his weight,
his invasion. His eyes glowed, tracking the slow, strong
slide of her fingers. He put his hands over hers, spread
her legs further, wider for him.

'Impatient, aren't you?' he murmured, his breath
teasing her as he moved closer.

But to her infinite relief and exquisite torture, he
bent his head and licked her there. A slow, lush taste.

She cried out, tightening her fingers on herself, hovering. 'Ruben.'

He lifted his head the merest fraction. 'Say—' a slide
of his finger '—my name again.'

'Ruben,' she whispered.

He blew a shot of warm tormenting air above, while
working his fingers inside. 'Say it again.'

'Ruben,' she pleaded, her body constricting.

His expression darkened. 'Scream it.' He bent forward and feasted.

She shrieked his name to the sky.

His hands remained hard on her thighs, mercilessly keeping her still for him, so he could continue applying his own brand of ecstatic torment. His tongue thrust deep, just as she wanted his erection to, or his fingers again, any part of him—just more. *All* of him. She threw her head back, her shriek not abating. Her hands clutched, trying to draw him closer. Wanting him to mount her, wanting him to ride her. Wanting it all harder than she ever had. Because she wanted as she never had. Oh, it was utter hedonism. She was spent, yet *starving*. She shook with the force of release, the savage orgasmic contractions going on and on. Until she begged over and over, 'I want you.'

He looked up, his fingers tracing back and forth softly across her slick, sensitive entrance. 'You want me to what?'

Panting, she swore at the amusement in his eyes. 'You know already.'

'How bad do you want it?'

She rocked harder into his hand. 'You know that already too.'

'I want you to tell me.'

He wanted it all? She reached, clenching his shoulders. 'Take me so hard I won't be able to walk.'

His cheeks flushed, his face went stern as determination gripped him. 'That hard?'

'Harder.' She wanted the furthest spectrum of pleasure. From him she'd settle for nothing less. This one night? This was all hers.

But he didn't rise and lie against her as she expected.

No, nothing was as she expected tonight. He stood and finally removed his boxers, got the protection.

She sat up, mouth watering. 'You want me to—'

'*No.*' A pained refusal. 'I won't last,' he growled.

He got onto the bed behind her, angling her slightly so they faced that reflection on the diagonal. He drew her to her knees, spreading them so his fitted between. His thighs were rock solid beneath hers. His erection strained against her soft flesh.

'Oh,' she gasped.

'Watch.'

She turned, gasped again at the erotic image in the window. She could see him behind her. His gaze met hers in that mirror. He held her waist firm in his hands and then encouraged her to rise up a little.

She did.

'Watch.' He leaned back, positioned her above him.

The instruction wasn't necessary—she couldn't tear her gaze from the sight of him thrusting upwards, from the sight of her swallowing him whole as he impaled her on him in one swift bite.

She screamed her joy. The excitement of watching their bodies fuse was too much. As was watching the play of his hand, now slipping down over her stomach to strum between her legs, the rippling of his thigh muscles as he flexed his hips, bumping her over and over, the sway of her own breasts—until he clutched them in his other palm. And then she watched the slide of his thumb over her nipples. She gasped for air, gasped to retain her sanity. And failed. Meeting his eyes in the reflection—she saw the glazed heat of lust that she felt mirrored within him too. The uncontrolled, animal lust. Until she couldn't watch any more. It was so overwhelming, she had to close her eyes to combat the intensity of the sensations. Because all this while, he was inside her, stroking deep, deep, deep inside her.

'Ellie,' he warned.

But she couldn't bear it any more. It was too hot, too intense—she just wanted another release *now*.

He moved. Lifting her, leaving her.

'*Ruben.*' She was furious, spun to face him, to pull him back.

But he pushed her down and, seeing the look on his face, she went, ecstatic. Lying back, panting, grateful for the cool cotton sheet beneath her. He loomed above, looking right into her eyes. There was no mistaking she was getting it all now.

All inhibition gone, all sense of reality gone, she smiled.

He held her apart, bent his head and kissed her. Then let her feel the immense power of him. She shook. This was what she'd wanted—his weight. *All* his weight pressing on her. Filling her. Almost smothering her with his strength. Her fingers spread, clutching his biceps, sliding round to his back to simply try to hang on. She arched her hips, trying to widen her legs more to cope with him. He owned her then. Thrusting again and again, filling her until her pleasure overflowed, releasing in harsh flashes, her nails digging, her screams raw as she revelled in his assault. She still couldn't get enough.

'Hell, you're demanding,' he choked. He gripped her hair and tilted her head back so he could see into her eyes. 'How much more do you want?'

'Every last damn bit,' she answered, throaty, unashamed, ravenous.

He threw back his head and thrust harder than ever. Slow and violent and so deep her groan was ripped from the core of her. It wasn't about fantasy any more; there was no game, no tease in his action. He was as unleashed, as uninhibited and as out of control as she. And she adored it.

Sweat slicked between their hot bodies. Skin sizzled where it touched, the burn such a pleasure she pushed closer still. Their movements deepened again, relentless, the pace now insane. She didn't want it to stop, never ever to stop. Yet she couldn't bear it a second longer.

He swore. 'I feel you, I can feel you—'

He broke off as her scream rose high, echoing round the unforgiving peaks of the mountains.

A long time later all she heard was his rough, rapid panting. His groan as he tried to control the frantic beat of his heart. Their sweat mingled. He was too heavy for her to push against. She didn't care. It was a heavenly way to suffocate.

With a pained moan he shifted slightly to the side. 'Can you breathe?'

'Just about.' Her throat was sore, she'd screamed so loud. Heat flooded her cheeks—not the lust kind. She'd been so *abandoned*.

He turned his head sharply. 'Don't regret a thing about it,' he said. 'Most awesome experience of my life.'

She nodded.

'It was even better than before,' he whispered. He shook his head hopelessly. 'All I want now is to do it all again. Again. Again.' He rolled right onto his back and growled up at the ceiling. 'But I have to catch my breath.'

And scratchy-voiced she reminded them both. 'Only tonight.'

CHAPTER TEN

HE WAS fitter than she, because he recovered far more quickly than she'd thought possible. But he was oh-*so*-kind, and let her just lie back while he explored. Deeply.

And then he leaned over her. 'Are you hungry?'

'You *can't* be serious.' She was aghast.

He roared with laughter. 'No, I mean your stomach.'

'Oh, that. Yes.'

He disappeared down the ladder and came back with long-life food. Yeah, muesli bars had never tasted so good.

'High energy.' He handed her a can. 'Drink that and have some chocolate. Not exactly gourmet but perfect given all that's required of you in the next ten hours.'

All that was required of her? Oh, she liked these demands. 'Aren't you planning to sleep at all?' She'd thought he'd been teasing about that, but now she wasn't so sure.

'Not a wink.'

Two hours later Ellie was *convinced* he'd want to sleep now. But the crazy thing was, although she was physically exhausted, the last thing she felt like was sleeping. 'Can we turn the lantern out?' she asked.

'No.' Ruben refused to let that happen. He didn't want to lose an hour of this to sleep.

'What if I promise to say your name, repeatedly, so you know I know who I'm with.'

He chuckled. 'Why do you want it out? You know we're not actually going to sleep any tonight.'

'I want to see the stars.'

He glanced at the big window. Okay, he could see how that would be good.

'I'll say your name lots.' She batted her eyelashes at him.

He knelt up and flicked the switch off. The moon wasn't big or terribly bright, but the white mass of stars was incredible.

She commando crawled to the end of the bed and leaned closer to the window. 'Ruben, this place is amazing.'

'I'm glad you like it.' He liked how she made him feel.

'Ruben, I don't just *like* it, up here we're practically in heaven. Ruben, this *is* heaven.'

Yeah, it was as close as he'd come to that.

'Ruben.' She said his name again in an exaggerated tease. 'Can you see *Lepus*?'

Given the way her eyes were reflecting the stars, he figured she meant a constellation. 'I can see the Southern Cross but that's about it.'

'Well, Ruben, if you look up there to the left, you'll see a bigger one, then three more in an almost circle around it,' she directed him. 'Do you see?'

'I think so,' he lied and heard her snort of disbelief. No fooling her, then.

But lying side by side staring up at the massive expanse of sky was nice. So was the way she played up the over-use of his name.

'Ruben, to the left.'

'Did your father teach you these?' he asked.

'Honestly, Ruben, he was more into the conquer-the-mountain thing. I learnt them myself. It was my personal reward for getting through the day's climb. Ruben, I'd lie there and look up at them and give thanks I made it through another day.'

'It really doesn't sound like fun.'

'It wasn't so bad, Ruben. At least I had him to myself for a bit, whereas Mum was always on the phone or something.'

Poor Ellie. Well, the least he could give her was his undivided, utterly focused attention—tonight.

He bit back the laughter at her repeat, repeat, repeat of his name. In the dark, lying sideways across the bed together, they looked at the stars. Somehow the conversation drifted. She joked her way through her assortment of odd jobs in the movie industry, then the focus turned to him—with her prompting he talked through the long, slow battle that had been the chateau. Ironic to think it had started with him begging any kind of work he could to get funds to develop it. He'd worked like a dog. Then all of a sudden success had snowballed. The acquisitions in recent years had him running faster than a hamster on speed—more hours than ever before. A week or so from one business to the next—he was driven to personally ensure each was on track. She listened in the dark, asked questions about the early years and commented, constantly beginning each utterance with his name.

And then she turned the clock back a year or so more and asked about his father—about the cancer. That dark period in his life when he'd lost his father and a few months later his mother had left.

Ruben rolled away but she wrapped her soft body around his and didn't let go.

'It's not something I can talk about,' he muttered beneath his breath.

She heard him. Softly whispered his name as she embraced him, refusing to let him shut off from her completely.

But he never ever discussed those days—had never admitted to anyone the heartbreak of nursing his terminally ill parent when his mother had been too tired and distraught to cope any more. He'd never unloaded the desolate loss, the helplessness, the hopelessness.

The kind of pain he never wanted to endure again. That unbearable loneliness.

'Ruben.' She whispered his name softly. Her voice, like her body, a caress—soothing and so very, very sweet. Somehow it was as if she understood and absorbed that deep, private hurt. And for the first time in his adult life Ruben relaxed into a loving embrace. She held him and he let her—until the melancholy moment suddenly passed and he could stand her quiet comfort no longer. It was something else he wanted from her, only that one thing—right?

'What are—? *Oh!*' Breathless, she forgot to say his name at the beginning of a sentence.

'Yeah.' He chuckled as she squealed again.

'What are you doing?' She managed to finish the sentence that time. Still sans his name.

'Turning the lantern back on.' He moved away quickly to do it.

'Why?'

He grabbed her by the legs and hauled her towards him. 'Because by the time I've done with you, you won't remember your *own* name, let alone mine.' It was that mindless pleasure he wanted. That beautiful, intense ecstasy.

Her star-filled eyes gleamed. 'Sounds fantastic.'

CHAPTER ELEVEN

Too few hours later Ellie woke. Blinking to banish the sleepy feeling, she frowned at the dull grey light. 'We've really fogged up the window.'

Ruben leaned across her to examine the glass. 'No, the fog is outside.'

'Really?' She sat up and swiped a finger across it. The grey remained. Clouds had descended, encompassing their tower. They couldn't see a thing.

'We can't fly out in this.' He sighed sleepily.

'But we can't stay here another night.' Panic threatened to drown her relaxed state as consciousness brought thought with it. One night she could manage. More was a definite no.

'We don't have a choice,' he replied. 'It's not safe to leave here until the fog lifts.'

Not safe physically perhaps, but this was her heart on the line. She'd let him in and more intimate time together would have her in trouble. She'd always known that. 'But—'

'Stop looking so worried.' He laughed roughly. 'We can't anyway. We're all out of condoms.'

'You're kidding.' Her jaw dropped.

He shook his head. 'It was only a three pack.'

How stupid had she been not to have any on her?

How stupid had he been not to buy in bulk? And had they really only had sex the three times? It felt like so much more. Mind you, there'd been other kinds of orgasms too.

'It's probably a good thing.' She closed her eyes and shook her head. 'This was enough.' Both her body and her heart were worn out. Now that fog just had to burn off super quick so she could keep as whole as possible and not leave that vital beating part of herself behind with him.

She felt him fall back on the pillows beside her. 'You're right.'

'I'm sorry?' She laughed, working up some humour to cover the sudden sense of devastation. She was learning tricks off him. 'Can you repeat that, please?'

'You're *right*,' he mumble grumbled.

'A little louder.'

He pulled the pillow out from under his head and threw it at her.

'Wow, a man who can admit when someone else—a woman—is right,' she teased, determined to jolly away the disappointment when she'd realised he couldn't come inside her again. And that for him this one night had truly been enough. 'Why haven't you been snapped up already?'

'Because I turn into a werewolf at full moon,' he teased back, reminding her of her old joke back that first morning after.

'Even more reason for you to have the ball and chain already. Women love a man in touch with his animal side,' she purred.

His brows lifted. 'You do like some animal in your man, don't you?'

She licked her lips and tipped her head back to utter a little howl.

He reached a long arm out and twisted his fingers into her hair. 'I like your hair like this. Neither straight or curly, but it definitely has this little kink.'

There was a time when Ellie would have ensured that every time she saw him next, her hair would be just so. She'd straightened it to a crisp for one boyfriend, curled it tight for another—always aiming to please. To do whatever to make a guy like her and keep liking her. Old habits died hard. But she wasn't going to do that for Ruben—it had never been that way between them and she wasn't going to slide backwards now. No, after last night she needed to make more than sure she stayed on top of her vulnerable trying-too-hard tendencies.

Despite only having a couple of hours' sleep in the early hours of the morning, she couldn't seem to get back to sleep now. Nor could Ruben. By unvoiced agreement they dressed and went downstairs, sat on the rug in front of the little log burner.

'We only have muesli bars left.' Ruben rummaged in the tin, pulling out packs of bars and bottled water. 'Sorry I don't have anything else.'

'I like muesli bars.'

'I don't even have a deck of cards,' he added ruefully.

'That's probably a good thing, I only know how to play poker.' Ellie glanced up and caught the look in his eye. Yeah, time to move the conversation along. 'I've got some news actually.'

Ruben took a bite out of his bar and chewed thoughtfully, taking satisfaction in the way her smile was bubbling out of her. That was his doing and it made him feel good.

'I'm up for a tourism award. Only a very minor one

of course. Rookie Guide of the Year—can you believe that?' She bounced on her knees. 'I've only been there a couple of months but I've been nominated! I'm so thrilled.'

So *that* was why she was glowing? It wasn't because she was still bathed in post-sex bliss? He felt stupidly deflated. 'That's awesome.' He nodded. 'When did you find out?'

'A few days ago,' she said.

A few days? But they talked on the phone every night. 'How come you didn't tell me already?' It niggled that she'd kept something so special a secret.

'I wanted to tell you in person.' She smiled, her pleasure iridescent. 'I wanted to see your reaction.'

'Oh.' He felt a bit better. 'Well, that's really cool. Good for you.'

'I've finally found what I'm meant to do.' She grinned and bit into her bar. 'It's the best job in the world.'

Impulse hit Ruben hard—he wanted to see if she won that award. He wanted to be there to give her a hug if she didn't. Okay, maybe he wanted to give her more than a hug. 'When do you find out if you've won?'

'There's a function—dinner and the awards and stuff—at the end of the week.'

'Do you get to take a date?'

She paused. 'I'm not sure.'

'If you do, will you take me?'

'You want to go?' She looked surprised and suddenly elated. The sun pierced through the clouds the same moment her smile exploded.

'Of course, that's what friends do.' He tried to get a grip. That was what this was about. Being a friend and supporter, right?

'Friends,' she echoed.

'We are still friends, right?' He blinked as the bright sunshine hurt his sleep-deprived eyes.

'Of course.' Her smile didn't dim.

Ruben was relieved the sun soon burned off the fog because he needed a little thinking space to assess quite where he was at. Satisfied, yes—but for how long? It was what she'd insisted on—one night—and then back to normal. But he really didn't feel quite right.

He flew them down to the airport—had booked her flight back to Wellington. He planned to stay at the lodge a couple of days and catch his breath. But when he said goodbye to her at the departures gate it was with a way-too-friendly, utterly breathless kiss. She melted into his arms and he unashamedly hauled her closer, revelling in her surrender. Maybe they'd take this one hook-up at a time. They could stay friends on the phone and lovers on the nights their schedules melded. No problem at all. And maybe their clashing out of town calendars could be just the thing to stop this affair from ending too soon.

Three days later Ellie was all but skipping around the office. She was supposed to be working on the plan for her next tour, but distraction in the form of random Ruben thoughts kept hitting her.

'You really can't concentrate, can you?' Bridie teased.

Fortunately her boss thought her dithering was about the awards tomorrow night, not the excitement of seeing Ruben again.

It was silly—he was coming tomorrow just as a friend. But she knew what might happen—he'd said it was enough, but that kiss goodbye at the airport?

Oh, she wanted more of that. She could control this added dimension to their friendship. Of course she could. Friends with benefits wasn't just a Hollywood set-up, maybe it could really work. Okay, so the realist in her sensed impending heartache, but there was that irrepressible flicker of hope—surely he wouldn't have offered to come with her if he didn't care even just a little, right?

Maybe, just maybe that wall of his was coming down—one brick at a time. They'd grown closer over the last few weeks—not physically but in all those phone calls. And then the physical had happened—and transported her to a whole other level. She'd never felt closer to anyone than she had with him in that hut. She'd never felt closer to heaven.

Ruben was staring at his calendar and planning future trips to Wellington for more nights with Ellie when his phone rang. It was a blocked number—and the call played to his innate ambition.

Anthony Mackenzie—of the Australian department store dynasty—was in the country with his sister. 'We'd love to have a meeting with you. We've heard you excel at discreet luxury.'

'Are you looking to stay at one of my venues?'

'We want you to come to Australia and build us some.'

Ruben paused for a 'wow' moment. Overseas expansion wasn't in his current plan but he'd be a fool not to make the connection. 'When did you want to meet?'

Ruben—still looking at his schedule—frowned as Anthony named the next day. It shouldn't matter—the meeting was in the afternoon, Ellie's gig was in the evening. So long as he made the flight he'd be there.

And if he missed the plane, he could charter his own. It wasn't going to be one of those clash of timing things at all. Fate wouldn't be so inconvenient. It was completely manageable.

The instant he hung up from Anthony, Ruben phoned Ellie. The opportunity made excitement burn all over and he wanted to share the buzz.

'Are you getting excited?' he teased her first when he heard an ultra-chirpy hello.

'No. I'm just going to relax and enjoy it. It's not about winning.'

Ruben smirked. It was *always* about winning. 'I've got a meeting in the afternoon.' Yeah, he was looking forward to the whole damn day.

'So you're not coming.' Not missing a beat, she leapt to the wrong conclusion. 'That's fine. I don't expect you to be there, I know you're really busy. If you can't make it that's cool.'

Something else burned in Ruben now. He paused, registering how effortless her shift to 'I don't mind' was. Had she *expected* him not to show? It had happened to her before, hadn't it? Her determined cheeriness to cover up any wound was too practised. Her parents probably. But Ruben didn't like that she trusted him so little.

'Of course I'm coming,' he said more sharply than he intended. 'I'll be flying in after. It's a short flight, you know. I'll be there.'

'You don't have to—'

'I want to, Ellie.' He sighed. 'Trust me.'

There was a moment of silence. 'Okay.' And then she finally asked, 'What's the meeting about?'

But the excitement of telling her about the connection

faded in the insecurity that whispered along the cellular network. 'Possibility of taking on a deal in Australia. New boutique hotels. Right from design stage.'

'Wow, that's big,' she said. 'That's really big.'

'It could be amazing.'

'Sure,' she agreed. 'But once you've nailed that, will it be enough?'

'What do you mean?'

'Once you've conquered Australia, what's next?'

'Indonesia maybe?' He ignored her underlying criticism and played up. 'Or Fiji?'

'Of course.' She sighed. 'You're going to end up with a massive chain.'

'No need to sound critical, you know I love a challenge.' And what would be so wrong with a massive challenge?

A small silence. 'Well, I hope the meeting goes really well. It sounds like it could be a great opportunity. And you're incredible at making the most of every opportunity that comes your way.'

He swallowed back the defence gagging in his throat. There was no point in fighting with her over the phone. Was she distancing—shoring up her defences in case he let her down?

Her determination not to care worried him. He didn't want to worry. He didn't want to have to mind how she might be feeling.

'So what are you planning to wear tomorrow?' He tried to tease them both out of it. 'The black slip dress would be good, with the sequined sandals.' He dreamed about that outfit all the time.

'You sound like my gay best friend, you know that?' she teased back.

He forced a chuckle but couldn't quite mask the bitter kernel burrowing deeper inside his chest. 'Isn't that what you wanted?'

Less than twenty-four hours later he shook hands with Anthony and Annabel Mackenzie—twin offspring of one of the wealthiest families in Australia. He was the playboy head of the department store conglomerate. She the former solo-sailing superstar. She was petite, beautiful and strong. He was tall and even stronger. Formidable competition, fantastic allies. Practically royalty. Ruben liked being his own boss, but he wasn't stupid. He'd forge a business alliance with the best of them. But only the best.

'Thanks for taking time out to meet us.' Anthony smiled.

'Pleasure,' Ruben replied. 'Thanks for the invitation.'

'We've been watching what you've been doing for a while,' Anthony said. 'We have some clients in common.'

Conversation quickly turned serious. They wanted him in on a consortium they were putting together to construct a couple of elite boutique lodges in Australia. Ruben would oversee it. But he wanted to know why they wanted him.

Annabel answered briskly. 'You're as driven as I am.'

'For different reasons.' They couldn't have more different backgrounds.

A smile showed her acknowledgement of that. 'You have the kind of focus that ensures success.'

He nodded slowly. Focus was everything. 'And you insist on success.'

'Absolutely.'

Yeah, this woman was driven. So was her steely-eyed brother. Ruben understood, he had that insatiable pit in his belly—the fire that needed constant fuel. They might have wildly different histories, but that commonality was there. And this would be some job. It wouldn't be days away, it would be *months*. It would be hours and hours of work. The kind of challenge Ruben relished.

'I'd need total control,' he said.

Anthony sat back and smiled. 'Naturally you would.'

As they talked Ruben glanced at Annabel. She was a woman well used to getting what she wanted, a beautiful, fit woman. A woman who had a lot in common with him. She had that ruthless, business-first ambition. Was the kind of person who'd made sacrifices—because no one could have it all. Especially those who dreamed big.

'I have the connections,' Anthony was saying. 'You design it.'

'We want your vision.'

But Ruben was struggling to concentrate and he'd *never* had trouble concentrating before. His work was everything to him. It had to be—for so long it had been all he'd had. No family, no friends, only wood and nails and garden had been the constants for him. He'd put his all into it and he'd reaped the benefits. As a kid it had been hard cultivating the 'I don't give a damn what you think' mentality, but now that attitude was second nature. It had seen him take massive risks that had paid off.

But Ellie's question circled—when would it be enough? Would it ever be enough? Or would the edge of dissatisfaction always be there?

He couldn't afford to care what Ellie thought. It limited him. He'd start to need approval and he'd needed approval from no one for decades. But he wanted to know what she thought of this. Her doubts made *him* doubt himself.

He agreed to research the idea and get back to them. Engrossed in thought, he took a taxi from their hotel for the airport. The Mackenzie siblings waved him off and for the first time Ruben felt his isolation keenly.

How could he feel lonely now?

He knew why and, damn it, he couldn't afford to be thinking about Ellie all the time. Couldn't afford to miss her. Couldn't afford to need to talk to her. She took up all his spare brain space. Plus the space he *didn't* have spare.

He didn't do relationships—not beyond superficial friendly or useful for business. None that required emotional investment. His business was his life. That was how he liked it and that was what made him happy. Thinking of her all the time was *not* making him happy.

He faced facts—it had to be over. He needed to cut her from his life so he could concentrate on what was most important to him. He'd tell her tonight, after the awards.

On a quiet Sunday morning, it could be only a twenty-minute drive to get to the airport, but in traffic like this it might be a good fifty minutes or more. His muscles clenched at the thought of seeing her again and having to say goodbye. He thought back on that conversation so late those few nights ago. The one that had turned him incandescent with rage and forced him into breaking the friendship boundary. His jaw clamped tighter but it was no use. He was powerless to resist, unable to block the constant dreams of her.

Starvation hadn't killed the sexual attraction. Nor had that night of indulgence. He thought of her more and more. Every phone call he heard the sultry in her voice.

Seeing her would only worsen it. So what was the point of tormenting himself even more? The sooner she was expunged, the better. And wouldn't seeing her once more only tempt him back into trouble?

The best idea would be for him to go to Australia as soon as possible and focus on that. Because what did she get from him really? He couldn't believe she really needed his friendship. She had plenty of other friends and she was already expecting him to let her down. Her reaction when he told her about the meeting had shown that. And even if, for just a second, he let himself dream of being with her, he knew he couldn't ask it of her. She loved her job. She was damn good at it. And it was completely incompatible with his. She didn't need him distracting her or holding her back. She'd been in it only a few months and she was up for an award already. It was her calling. What she was best at, and what she adored. She was becoming as bad a workaholic as he was.

He frowned at that. She was tired with all these back to back tours. She needed a rest. In his most private dream he'd take her back to the hut and pin her there until she'd caught up on all the sleep she needed. He groaned at the agony. Because it wasn't really sleep he was dreaming of.

And then he thought back to that call—the 'it's okay to meet someone else' call. Wasn't her staying 'friends' with him limiting her chances of meeting other people? Couldn't there be some guy she'd meet who'd be so much better for her? Some other tour guide or some-one who had more to offer her. It would happen soon enough. There'd be some charmer on her tour who'd tempt her. Who'd treat her the way she ought to be treated.

He didn't want to be on the end of the phone when she told him about her new lover. Never.

He'd hurt Sarah with his unavailability. His 'lack of support' as she'd put it. Emotional—not financial, of course. He didn't want to hurt Ellie. Not any more than he had to. There was no future for their friendship. It couldn't ever work. It wasn't working *now*. And he couldn't bear the thought of feeling hurt himself. The sooner it was over, the better for the both of them.

He leaned forward in the seat and called to the driver. 'Actually, I've changed my mind. Turn back to the city, please.' He'd check into a hotel and get to work researching the Australians' proposal. That was his future.

He fished out his phone. He didn't want to speak to her. Not with this ache in his upper chest as if he were coming down with some infection—he didn't want her to hear him sounding husky. He'd text her. He stared sightlessly at the screen, deciding how to word it. Best to end it in a way that would be complete for her. To do what she expected in her heart. He paused, motionless.

He wasn't looking out of the window. He never saw the car at the intersection—the one not slowing down for the light as it should. He never heard the noise. Because at that moment, the only thing he could see was her sparkling eyes.

Ellie didn't wear the black slip dress. She went all out and bought a new one—that she couldn't really afford and that she'd probably wear only the once because it was too *luxe* for everyday life. French navy in colour, clingy—she felt a million dollars wearing it. Not to mention sensual, with cool silk skimming over her skin. Not that she was thinking sex either.

She did her make-up, blow-dried her hair, slipped her feet into the kind of shoes she could only bear to wear for minutes rather than hours—the sparkly, insane stiletto sort, with heels so high she'd be practically *en pointe*. But it would be fine—dinner was a sit-down affair, she'd taxi there. And Ruben would still be taller than her but she might be able to brush her lips over his with a mere tilt of her chin.

Of course, she took her imagination in a firm grip, she'd be brushing her lips across his cheek, not his mouth. They were *friends*. And she was not, not, *not* counting the hours until she saw him again. Absolutely did *not* know exactly how many seconds it had been since she last saw him.

'Oh, wow, you look amazing.' Bridie smiled at her when Ellie made it to the bar.

The venue for the awards was a couple of doors along. Ruben was coming straight from the airport. A hot flare of desire burst inside her at the mere thought of seeing him. She shivered, telling her skipping heart to calm down.

'You need another drink?' she asked Bridie, needing to move to work off some of her nervous energy.

She went to the bar, checked her phone while waiting to be served. No message. She was still giving herself a mental lecture even after the bartender had poured the drinks and she was carrying them back to the group. There could be traffic delays, flight delays, all kinds of reasons why he wasn't there yet. Twenty minutes later she bit the bullet and sent him a text.

Just 2 let u know we've gone into the convention centre for the awards. Yr name is on the door so u can get in, but let me know when u get here & I'll meet u.

She sat at the table. Silly to be nervous. Her hands

cold and clammy, her heart skipping beats uncomfortably. Restless. Time played with her mind—two minutes felt like twenty. A permanent state of waiting was a horrible way to live.

And then time sped up. The awards were all on and she wanted the clock hands to slow again. It wasn't as if she could ask them to delay the announcements. It was okay. She had Bridie on one side of her. An empty seat on the other but, hey, that didn't really matter—not when there were canapés to die for and an endless amount of wine. And a bunch of flirty tourism types who truly knew how to party.

'Do you think he's going to make it?' Bridie asked.

Ellie smiled with a careless shrug and was so glad she'd played down her relationship with Ruben. A friend, she'd defined him herself, right? She checked her phone again. Still no message. He didn't even have the decency to reply to her text?

'I don't know that he is.' She turned away so Bridie couldn't see her screen and lied to cover the fact she'd been stood up. 'Oh, no, his flight's been delayed.'

But she'd used her phone to check the airport website only ten minutes before—all flights were on schedule and operating normally. If he'd got the flight he'd be here already. And if he hadn't got the flight, why hadn't he contacted her to let her know?

Goosebumps feathered over her skin.

She knew why he hadn't contacted her. Because he didn't want to be there. If he'd really wanted to be there, he'd be there. It was like all those unfulfilled promises of her parents. One or other would promise to be there—a sports day, a special assembly—but more often than not they'd forget, too swept up in their own affairs, careers or better offers. Once or twice one or other had arrived just at the end—having missed her event. Never on time. Never truly there just for her. Something or someone else always came first.

And so it was with Ruben. For him work came first. It always would. And that was okay if she could put up with it. But she didn't want to put up with it. She didn't want to be second best. Just for once she wanted to be put first in someone's life. But that someone wasn't going to be Ruben.

That secret, hidden dream shattered.

What an absolute fool she'd been. He'd utterly played her with his acquiescence to her friendship request, with his phone calls and supposed sharing. He'd only been after the one thing—and he'd got it that night up in the mountain. There hadn't been any kind of amazing more-than-physical connection for him, there'd just been sex.

How naïve to think he'd show up tonight. How naïve to think a friendship could work. How point-blank stupid of her to have said yes to any damn benefits.

And how it hurt. It hurt worse than any of those damn sports days or disappointments from her parents. She'd given her heart and got nothing back. But she was determined to hide it—even from herself. She was damn well determined to have a good night out.

When it came to announcing the winner of the category she was nominated in, someone else's name was called. Someone else went up and collected their award. Ellie smiled lots and clapped loudly. Then she sipped some of that wine, ate another canapé and conversed enthusiastically with all those around her.

She *should* have been an actress—she could mask misery so easily.

But she went out with her colleagues, determined to find comfort in company. She'd hang with her true friends. And Ruben wasn't one of them.

CHAPTER TWELVE

RUBEN's head ached really badly. So did the rest of him. He was alone—just as he'd always believed he wanted. And, hell, he'd been wrong.

Sure there were people he could call. All those names in his contacts file—he could get any one of his 'friends' and they'd be there in a flash. But what would they do? Sit and talk sport or weather or politics? Not one of them really *knew* him—and he didn't really know them. He'd kept a certain distance so well it was second nature. And now he realised how alone it had made him.

Because there was one person who'd slipped through those barriers. One person he ached to see. One person whose comfort he wanted. Someone whose arms he wanted around him—someone he wanted to confide every last little thing to. Someone he'd been trying to contact for the last three days.

She didn't answer her phone. He rang five, ten, fifty times and every call went to the answer service. He tried ringing from a land-line so she wouldn't recognise the number. Still she didn't take the call.

So now he knew the reality of this new life. Accident or not, this would have happened anyway. He'd have finished that text and sent it, so the result would have been the same. She'd have been avoiding him. There'd be no contact.

And accident or not, he'd still be this bruised. Yeah, it wasn't those real cuts and bruises bleeding him, but that damn muscle in his chest. The injury that he had sole responsibility for and that radiated agony throughout the rest of him.

He was an idiot. A powerless idiot. Stuck in a hospital bed with an IV needle deep in his arm and cracked ribs that meant an airline wouldn't take him onboard. Not as far as Australia, so he couldn't escape as he'd planned to. But he couldn't escape anyway, aeroplane policy or not. He wanted to take it all back and start again. And while he might not be able to get on a plane, he could get into a campervan with a driver. He'd lie down most of the way, but he wasn't living through another day without trying to make things right. He'd been acting the coward too long as it was.

Ellie had a new phone—a very cute new smart phone that she could download a zillion apps on. She was just deciding which music to set as her ringtone when it rang with a real call. She didn't recognise the number. 'Hello?'

'Are you through punishing me?' he asked bluntly. 'Are you ready to talk to me yet?'

All kinds of emotions tumbled through Ellie. For a moment she couldn't cope with the spike in adrenalin that boosted the performance of every vital organ. 'I've been busy,' she finally breathed.

'This is how you treat your friends? Why have you been ignoring my calls?'

'I haven't been. I lost my phone.' Okay, so she'd thrown it in Wellington harbour. Not the most adult thing to have done but, hey, she'd got glum in the wee small hours after the chaotic clubbing scene of the awards after party.

'Good of you to give me your new number.'

How he'd managed to get it she didn't know.

He sighed. 'Can you just be mad with me, please? Just yell or something.'

She sat in a ball on the floor because her legs wouldn't work any more. 'There's nothing to yell about, Ruben. I'm fine.'

'Really?'

'Sure,' she said, pride surging. 'I'm not in some kind of decline just because you didn't turn up when you said you would. I had a really good night actually—it was quite a party.'

'I saw the photos on the company's Facebook page. I saw some others from the last tour too.'

'Yeah,' she reminisced with a fake smile that she hoped would sound real down the phone. 'They were a bit of a wild bunch.'

'And you had a good time with them.'

'It's my job to help them have a good time.'

'More Scotsmen.'

'What can I say? I seem to attract them.'

In one of those pictures she'd been wearing a Scottish flag and very little else. They'd had a toga party. It had been fun. There'd been bare-chested men in kilts. Nothing had happened with any of them, of course, but just the flirtation had made her feel better, right? She'd been popular. No matter that it was only temporary—for the two-day tour duration. She knew how to please people. But she'd once told Ruben that she didn't feel as if she had to please him. She wasn't going to please him now. She drew in a breath, dug up that deep resolve. 'You know this "let's be friends" deal?'

'Uh-huh.'

'It's not working for me.'

'Why not?'

'Well.' She screwed her eyes closed as she went for brutal honesty. 'I'm not going to meet anyone else when I'm still being "friends" with you.' She held her breath, heard his whistle in.

'You really want to meet someone else?'

'I think that would be the best thing for me, yeah.' Her toes curled and her skin goosebumped in revulsion at the thought of it. But it *was* the best thing. Ruben didn't want her beyond an occasional bed buddy and she didn't want to be mooning over him for the next millennia. She had to be kind to herself and cruel at the same time, because sending him away was hard.

'You're not even going to say this to my face?'

'Nope. I'm doing it over the phone. You're lucky it wasn't a text. It nearly was.' His mere presence was enough to tempt her. One smile enough to keep her hope afloat for weeks. She wanted to fall *out* of love with him. The cold turkey approach was the only way that could possibly work.

'Is this because I missed the show?'

'Oh, wow, you think?' Yeah, she'd just lost her grip on cool and capable.

'Ellie—'

'You don't have to explain it. I understand. You don't care for me.'

Silence. Then he got snappy right back at her. 'Our "friendship" isn't a one-way street, Ellie. You haven't been the best of friends to me either, you know.'

Well, that wasn't fair. But she was too hurt to argue.

The last thing she wanted to face was the fact that she loved his calls, loved hearing his tales. She got more than he did from this and she wanted more still. 'I don't think we were ever truly friends, Ruben. I think all those movies are right—men and women can't do platonic friendship. Let's call it a day, okay?'

She jabbed the end-call button, furiously blinking back the sting of rejection.

Someone instantly started hammering down her front door. She swiped the trickles from her cheeks and stormed the stairs. The door was rattling in the frame. She yanked it open. 'You were outside all this time?'

'I've had enough of the phone call rubbish.' He barged in, plucking her phone from her hand as he pushed past and flinging it across the room. His went with it.

Stunned, she watched them smash on the floor. 'You've probably broken both of them!'

'Good. So we're forced to speak face to face.'

She turned back and stared at him. For the second time that night her knees went completely weak. 'What the hell happened?'

'Car crash.'

Her lungs then failed too. 'You're kidding,' she wheezed.

'No. On the way to the airport the night of your awards.'

That was why he hadn't turned up? That was four days ago. 'And you're still this bruised?' He looked *awful*. Not even the jeans and the favourite 'Lucky' shirt could lift his near death-mask look. 'Why didn't you try to get in touch with me?' She was so shocked she shouted.

'When I regained consciousness the next day I did try. Just went to your answerphone.'

Oh, now she felt terrible. He'd had an accident—a horrible accident that could have been so much worse. And she hadn't been there for him. He'd been alone and abandoned again. That just broke her heart. But how was she to have known if he didn't tell her?

Ruben had decided on the trip down that he was going to fight hard—and dirty. No matter how, he was winning this woman.

'Friends are supposed to look out for each other,' he snapped, belligerent. Mad with himself as much as he was with her. 'Why didn't you call me to see where I was?'

'I sent you a text,' she snapped, equally defensive.

'One.' His hurt spilled. 'You never followed up. You never called that night or the next day. If we were such great friends how could you walk away so easily?' He breathed in and it hurt. Every breath hurt.

'So this is my fault?'

It was *all* her fault. 'You didn't care about me enough to wonder where I was or whether I was okay.'

She paled; her blue eyes weren't sparkling, but glistening. 'It never occurred to me you might not be okay.'

'No, you just thought the worst of me. That I'd let you down.' He breathed in hard and honesty—responsibility—slammed into him. Because he knew exactly why she'd not followed up with her call—she'd been afraid, yet certain, of his rejection. 'And you were right, that's exactly what I'd decided to do.'

Yeah, his chest burned. He saw the horror in her eyes at the sight of his bruises. But he couldn't win this that dirty after all. He didn't want to win her through sympathy. Her guilt was a hollow, bitter victory. He didn't want pity. He didn't want her to feel bad or obligated. He just wanted her to love him the way he loved her. But she deserved the truth. Even if it meant he might lose her.

'The accident doesn't matter,' he said huskily. 'I wasn't going to be there anyway.'

'What do you mean you weren't going to be there?' She'd backed up to the wall, as far from him as she could get.

'I'd decided to end it. I was texting you to say I wasn't coming when the accident happened.'

'You were texting while driving?' she screeched, anger flooding back.

'Actually I was in the back of a taxi.'

She stared at him and as the seconds ticked he didn't just see the pain he'd inflicted on her, he felt it himself. Her hurt was his—because his heart was hers.

'Why are you telling me this?' Ellie had suffered too many shocks already. She didn't get what the guy wanted or why he was here.

'I want to be honest with you. I want to clear this up.'

Clear it up? As in *over*? Hadn't she just tried to do that? What was with the torment?

'I don't want to be friends with you, Ellie. I want a relationship with you.' He looked less than impressed about it. 'I can't get you out of my head,' he growled.

She had no sympathy—nothing left to give in the face of this. 'Maybe you need to try harder.'

'Ellie.' He shook his head, his voice low. 'I can't stay away from you.'

'You can't stay away from *sex*. That's all it is.'

'No, that is not all it is,' he shouted back. 'We hadn't had sex in *weeks*.' He drew breath—the damn cracked rib kept poking him, forcing the honesty. 'Yes, that was a big part of it at first. But then it was you. *All* of you.'

She wasn't buying it. 'You only did the calls because you were frustrated that I hadn't put out. I was the challenge—and once you'd conquered me up on that mountain you weren't interested any more.'

'That's not true.'

'Well, what is it you want from me, then?' Oh, she hurt. So hurt. But she couldn't be second best. Not when he'd become her everything.

'Ellie.' His voice broke. He leaned back against her door, his body completely rigid, every muscle straining as he pressed his fists to his chest. 'I can't sleep. I'm barely eating. I can't concentrate on anything at work. I haven't for weeks. I don't want to be this *obsessed*. I've always been totally one track, but, now, *you're* the track. And I can't fight it any more. I don't care about anything else. All I care about is being with you.' He scrubbed his hands through his hair. 'But I've never had a relationship actually work for more than five minutes. And I can't...' He sighed. 'You deserve more than I can give you.'

Ellie stared at him—stunned and uncomprehending. 'Why do you think you can't give me what I need?'

'I've never been able to before,' he said harshly. 'And I've never wanted to. I hate feeling so out of control.' He straightened away from the door, and awkwardly walked to her lounge. 'My parents' relationship limited them. Neither achieved their ambitions. Dad had his dreams but they hardly got off the ground. They were too tied up with each other.'

'Is that so bad?'

'I know they were happy,' he admitted. 'And maybe because of the way the world viewed them they were an even tighter unit. But it was frustrating.' He hobbled about her lounge, not looking at her. 'We came out here when I was six. I had this French accent, an ancient dad and I loved him. But he bought this wreck of a property and said he was going to turn it into a *chateau*.' Ruben laughed painfully. 'He drew up these awesome plans. But that was about as far as he got.'

'So you did it for him.' Ellie knew this but she thought she had it all now. 'But you really think their relationship held your father back from achieving anything else?'

He winced. 'Not just him, they were both hopeless that way. No one can have it all. And if you want to do something you're better to be free to get on with it.'

'But maybe neither of them *wanted* to achieve those dreams that much. Maybe your father was just enjoying being a husband and a dad—you said yourself he never thought it was going to happen. Maybe he wanted to spend that time *imagining* his dreams with you—rather than *not* spending that time with you as he made them a reality. I'm sure he'd be thrilled with what you've done, but I don't know that he'd be so pleased with how you've isolated yourself to do it.'

He was silent a long moment. She could see the shifting emotions in him—saw the hopelessness lift.

But then he turned away. 'My ex resented the time I put into work. It came to a head—I had to pick her or the deal for the Taupo lodge. I chose the deal and she walked. At the time I was glad. But this time?' He shook his head. 'I don't want to hurt you like that. I don't want to lose you but how can I be fair to you?'

'But I'm not her. I want to *support* you, not hold you back.' She'd love to help him however she could. 'And

I want you to support me. Why can't we achieve our dreams together?'

He jerked his head, turning back to face her. 'You're the first woman I've ever put before work, the only woman who's made work seem utterly meaningless.' He walked towards her. 'You're the only woman I've chased. And I'm going to keep chasing as long as I have to.'

It wasn't going to have to be for much longer. Her eyes filled with tears.

'Ellie, you're everything and more to me.' He stopped in front of her. 'You don't need to be anything other than yourself. You're the perfect woman for me.' He stepped close enough to touch—so he only had to whisper. 'Just you. Just as you are. I need you in my life. I never knew how much I needed you until I tried to live without you.'

'This is you chasing, huh?' She swiped the streaming rivers from her cheeks.

'This is me being honest,' he said softly. 'I didn't want to hurt you but I did and I'm so sorry. But I didn't want to hurt myself either and I thought walking away would save me from that. I was so wrong.' His voice softened. 'Because the thing is, I *am* like my parents. I love as deeply. You. I *hate* being apart from you. I want to be with you all of the time. I don't want to go away. I don't want you going away from me.' He shook his head. 'It's crazy. I think about you all the time. I miss you like you wouldn't believe. It *hurts*. It's a physical ache. I never wanted to hurt like this.'

Oh, she knew that ache. The constant, incurable gnawing deep inside. The coldness in bed—despite summer heat or electric blankets. The sadness at the stretch of bed beside her. The inadequacy of a quick phone call. The inability to catch his eye, to smile at a joke she knew he'd get. She missed that magic language, that connection that she'd never had with another person. Only him. It was real heartache, that heaviness of his absence. He wasn't hers and she'd thought he couldn't ever be. Oh, that had hurt.

'I feel for you like I've never felt for anyone. I've fought it. I thought I could control it, but I can't. I just want to be with you.' He took her hand in his. 'I don't want to go anywhere else. Home is where you are.' He looked intently into her eyes. 'You're the most important thing in my life.'

She nodded. Swallowed. Trying to clear the blurring in her eyes, the building of emotion in her throat.

'That's the nicest thing anyone's ever said to me.' Her throat was so constricted from holding back her emotion that it was hardly a whisper that sounded. She put her fingers to her lips to stop the sobs from ripping free.

'Please let me love you,' he whispered back. 'I'll do whatever I have to.'

'You don't have to do anything *but* love me,' she whispered. 'I don't want you giving up things that are important to you.'

'I'm not.'

'What about those Australians?'

'The terrible twins?' He laughed. 'They'll find someone else. I'm not in the market for global domination. Just national.'

'Really?'

'I have lots of things to do round here—at work and with you.'

She smiled. 'So do I. Planning to be the best tour guide in the country, you know.'

'Of course.' He nodded. 'So maybe I could come on

tour sometimes?' That one eyebrow went even higher. 'I could learn all those lines and achieve Ultra Fan Status.'

She chuckled—well, it was more a hiccup. Because she didn't know if she could handle his presence when she was leading a tour. 'You might be too much of a handful on my bus.'

He winked. 'I do solemnly declare that I will never manhandle you on tour time. Only in the hotel every night.'

'It's not you I'm worried about.' She smiled. It was her own urges. 'But maybe I could travel with *you* sometimes?'

'Any time you want. I won't visit the lodges as much. I need to consolidate and I could stay in town more. Here.'

'You're going to move in with me?' Her eyebrow took the upwards escalator that time.

'If you'll have me.' He paused.

'Is it going to be enough for you?' What if he got bored and felt she was holding him back?

'I'm talking long-term commitment, Ellie. I'm talking life. Literally. I want a family,' he said softly.

'You're talking kids?' Her voice lifted a dozen octaves. *And* he'd used the C-word?

'And I want to be involved.' He nodded, seeming to miss her total astonishment. 'I don't want them turning themselves inside out to get my attention. I don't want to do that to our children. I want them to know how important they are.'

The security she *hadn't* been given by her parents. Knowing he understood that made her melt completely. She leaned against his chest. 'I think if you tell them…'

He shook his head. 'Words aren't enough,' he whispered. 'It's all in the actions. Words mean nothing if they're not backed up with action. I want to *show* them. Just as I want to show you.'

'You already have.'

'No, I've only just begun. I love you, Ellie. Let me show you how for the rest of our days.'

Not often did an actual climax live up to the fantasy of Ellie's unlimited—heavily Hollywood influenced—imagination. This moment wasn't like that. There was no cinematic tweaking, no flash mob dancing, no proposals in neon lights… But nothing could beat the sincerity shining in the light in his eyes. Nothing could beat the liquid joy racing in her veins. Nothing could stop her from smiling, from crying. She squeezed her eyes shut as her tears flowed faster. Warmth seeped into her skin—the feel of his skin, his strong body, his tight embrace. Yes, the blaze of passion was there, but it was based on an eternal flame, a lick of heat that was all security. All his love.

She'd never felt so treasured. So wanted. In every way that mattered. In that most special of ways. She was his partner in everything. His equal. And they were going to work it *together*.

'I love you.' She'd give him everything she had to give. It could never be too much, now she understood that. He wanted it all—wanted to give her the same.

He groaned. 'I need you.'

She couldn't believe he was so blown away to have her in his arms. That he too was so ecstatic and so relieved that she'd opened up to him. As if he'd really believed she might not.

He moved, lifting her.

'This is a bad idea,' she yelped. 'You're injured.'

'I'm fine,' he argued.

'You're not.'

'Hold me back any longer and I won't be. Please let me do this.'

She cupped his cheek with her hand. 'Only if you let me take care of you too.'

He smiled at her—that lucky, lovely smile—and carried her to the place they both needed to be. She muffled her gasps when she saw the extent of his bruising, but he'd already seen her distress.

'It looks worse than it is.'

'Liar.' She brushed a kiss over the purplish skin near his ribs.

'I love you.'

'We haven't had sex this simple,' she said softly as he carefully moved over her.

'This isn't simple,' he answered. 'And this isn't sex.'

She arched instinctively, her neck, her spine, her feet. Every muscle clenched on the pleasure of him, breathing hard already. Abandoned moans were a mere thrust away.

'This is love.' His biceps rippled as he braced over her, pausing before driving his point home. 'This is making love.'

She cried, 'Oh, yes.'

He groaned and pulled back, trying to slow down. 'It's not going to be a marathon.'

'Not a problem.' She arched again, the ripples starting already.

His grin was lopsided and strained. And so lucky. Their eyes met—vulnerable, revealing. Trusting.

In the aftermath he nuzzled closer, his weight so wonderfully heavy on her. She blew cool, teasing air over his face and neck.

'I think I'm the luckiest guy ever,' he whispered gruffly.

She looked at the lamp where his tee shirt had landed and saw the old slogan and smiled, the most secure and certain of anything in her life. 'Yeah,' she whispered. 'There's no one luckier than you. Except me.'

She felt his smile against her skin.

'We're going to spend the rest of our lives arguing that,' he teased.

Pure happiness radiated through her. She softened. His completely. Happy completely.

'I know.'

EPILOGUE

One Year Later.

'I'M NOT going to win, you know. Just to be nominated is amazing. I never expected it, not two years in a row.'

Scepticism was painted all over Ruben's face. 'Just to be nominated? No one actually believes that, you know. Everyone wants to win. You included.'

Ellie determinedly shook her head. 'It would be nice to win, but I'm not going to be devastated if I don't. I'm going to enjoy the night anyway.' She'd partied like a wild woman last year when she hadn't won. This year was going to be so much better than that because he was with her and they'd just had the best year ever.

'You are?'

She nodded. 'You by my side, a job I adore. Life can't get better.'

Those gorgeous lips of his curved a little deeper. 'I got you a little something.'

'A consolation prize?' She giggled. 'To make me feel better if I don't win?'

'I wouldn't say it's a consolation prize. But it's for later.'

'Can I have it now?' She sent him a flirt look.

'Your category hasn't even been announced yet.'

'I don't care.' She leaned close, brushing against him. 'I'm far more interested in what you've got for me.'

'It really is for later.'

'Please?'

He sighed. 'I can't say no to you.' He put his hand in his pocket. 'But hopefully you can't say no to me either.'

He opened his hand in front of her.

Ellie looked at the box. The noise of the crowded room was suddenly muted. The crowd had vanished too—she was conscious of only him and her. 'Oh, Ruben.'

'Bit of an odd place to do this, but...'

She looked up. She could see only him—his gorgeous brown eyes, that charming, lucky smile and the love that shone through.

'You'll say yes? You'll marry me?'

'Of course I will,' she said. Only she was so choked up with emotion it was little more than a whisper.

She didn't hear her name over the sound system, she was so busy kissing him.

It was Bridie who poked her in the back and informed her she'd just won Tour Guide of the Year.

She hit the stage, collected her award and was heading back to her seat with no recollection whatsoever of what she'd said or done. But the entire audience had laughed and cheered so it must have been okay. And he was waiting with eyes only for her and with all the love she could ever want.

She ran the last few steps into his embrace. Real life was so much better than anything Hollywood could conjure. And Ellie Summers had won her world.

* * * * *

Mills & Boon® Hardback

June 2012

ROMANCE

A Secret Disgrace	Penny Jordan
The Dark Side of Desire	Julia James
The Forbidden Ferrara	Sarah Morgan
The Truth Behind his Touch	Cathy Williams
Enemies at the Altar	Melanie Milburne
A World She Doesn't Belong To	Natasha Tate
In Defiance of Duty	Caitlin Crews
In the Italian's Sights	Helen Brooks
Dare She Kiss & Tell?	Aimee Carson
Waking Up In The Wrong Bed	Natalie Anderson
Plain Jane in the Spotlight	Lucy Gordon
Battle for the Soldier's Heart	Cara Colter
It Started with a Crush...	Melissa McClone
The Navy Seal's Bride	Soraya Lane
My Greek Island Fling	Nina Harrington
A Girl Less Ordinary	Leah Ashton
Sydney Harbour Hospital: Bella's Wishlist	Emily Forbes
Celebrity in Braxton Falls	Judy Campbell

HISTORICAL

The Duchess Hunt	Elizabeth Beacon
Marriage of Mercy	Carla Kelly
Chained to the Barbarian	Carol Townend
My Fair Concubine	Jeannie Lin

MEDICAL

Doctor's Mile-High Fling	Tina Beckett
Hers For One Night Only?	Carol Marinelli
Unlocking the Surgeon's Heart	Jessica Matthews
Marriage Miracle in Swallowbrook	Abigail Gordon

Mills & Boon® Large Print

June 2012

ROMANCE

An Offer She Can't Refuse	Emma Darcy
An Indecent Proposition	Carol Marinelli
A Night of Living Dangerously	Jennie Lucas
A Devilishly Dark Deal	Maggie Cox
The Cop, the Puppy and Me	Cara Colter
Back in the Soldier's Arms	Soraya Lane
Miss Prim and the Billionaire	Lucy Gordon
Dancing with Danger	Fiona Harper

HISTORICAL

The Disappearing Duchess	Anne Herries
Improper Miss Darling	Gail Whitiker
Beauty and the Scarred Hero	Emily May
Butterfly Swords	Jeannie Lin

MEDICAL

New Doc in Town	Meredith Webber
Orphan Under the Christmas Tree	Meredith Webber
The Night Before Christmas	Alison Roberts
Once a Good Girl...	Wendy S. Marcus
Surgeon in a Wedding Dress	Sue MacKay
The Boy Who Made Them Love Again	Scarlet Wilson

Mills & Boon® Hardback

July 2012

ROMANCE

The Secrets She Carried	Lynne Graham
To Love, Honour and Betray	Jennie Lucas
Heart of a Desert Warrior	Lucy Monroe
Unnoticed and Untouched	Lynn Raye Harris
A Royal World Apart	Maisey Yates
Distracted by her Virtue	Maggie Cox
The Count's Prize	Christina Hollis
The Tarnished Jewel of Jazaar	Susanna Carr
Keeping Her Up All Night	Anna Cleary
The Rules of Engagement	Ally Blake
Argentinian in the Outback	Margaret Way
The Sheriff's Doorstep Baby	Teresa Carpenter
The Sheikh's Jewel	Melissa James
The Rebel Rancher	Donna Alward
Always the Best Man	Fiona Harper
How the Playboy Got Serious	Shirley Jump
Sydney Harbour Hospital: Marco's Temptation	Fiona McArthur
Dr Tall, Dark...and Dangerous?	Lynne Marshall

MEDICAL

The Legendary Playboy Surgeon	Alison Roberts
Falling for Her Impossible Boss	Alison Roberts
Letting Go With Dr Rodriguez	Fiona Lowe
Waking Up With His Runaway Bride	Louisa George

0612 GEN STD HB

ROMANCE

Roccanti's Marriage Revenge	Lynne Graham
The Devil and Miss Jones	Kate Walker
Sheikh Without a Heart	Sandra Marton
Savas's Wildcat	Anne McAllister
A Bride for the Island Prince	Rebecca Winters
The Nanny and the Boss's Twins	Barbara McMahon
Once a Cowboy...	Patricia Thayer
When Chocolate Is Not Enough...	Nina Harrington

HISTORICAL

The Mysterious Lord Marlowe	Anne Herries
Marrying the Royal Marine	Carla Kelly
A Most Unladylike Adventure	Elizabeth Beacon
Seduced by Her Highland Warrior	Michelle Willingham

MEDICAL

The Boss She Can't Resist	Lucy Clark
Heart Surgeon, Hero...Husband?	Susan Carlisle
Dr Langley: Protector or Playboy?	Joanna Neil
Daredevil and Dr Kate	Leah Martyn
Spring Proposal in Swallowbrook	Abigail Gordon
Doctor's Guide to Dating in the Jungle	Tina Beckett